GOLDEN CRUMBS

Mary Ruefle is the author of many books, including *The Book*, *Dunce*, which was a finalist for the 2020 Pulitzer Prize, *My Private Property*, *Trances of the Blast*, *Madness, Rack, and Honey*, a finalist for the National Book Critics Circle Award in Criticism, and *Selected Poems*, winner of the William Carlos Williams Award from the Poetry Society of America. She is the recipient of numerous honours, including the Robert Creeley Award, an Award in Literature from the American Academy of Arts and Letters, a Guggenheim fellowship, a National Endowment for the Arts fellowship and a Whiting Award. She lives in Bennington, Vermont, where she was poet laureate from 2019–2024.

CONTENTS

GOLDEN CRUMBS

MARY RUEFLE

'Mary Ruefle is the kind of poet who can make Tupperware seem transcendent.'
— Emily Berry, author of *Unexhausted Time*

'Ruefle is perceptive and reflective, silly and laugh-out-loud funny. She is like a saint of language and her collections are like prayer books.... I return to them again and again for nourishment.'
— Rachel Hurn, *Music & Literature*

'Ruefle is the Poet Laureate of the City of Ideas – surreal and lyrical and deeply moving at the same time.'
— Michael Klein, *Los Angeles Review of Books*

'Ruefle is clearly one of the best American poets writing, and her body of work is remarkable for its spiritual force, intelligence, stylistic virtuosity and adventurousness.'
— Tony Hoagland, *On the Seawall*

'Mary Ruefle's careful, measured sentences sound as if they were written by a thousand-year-old person who is still genuinely curious about the world.... She combines imagistic techniques from surrealism with narrative techniques to create surprising, high-velocity and deeply affecting work. This aesthetic has spawned many imitators and variations, but her style is unmistakable.'
— *The Stranger*

'A poet of visionary imagination, abiding sensitivity and melancholy humour.'
— *Publishers Weekly*

'For more than thirty years, [Ruefle] has freshened American poetry by humbly glorifying both the inner life and the outward experience.'
— Rodney Jones, *Poetry Society of America*

Praise for *The Most of It*

'By turns droll, witty, heartfelt and fanciful the pieces in *The Most of It*, whatever you choose to call them, offer something for every taste and temperament, which seems only fitting for a book that is dedicated "TO YOU."'
— Kathleen Rooney, *Boston Review*

'These very short pieces are like butter mints wrapped in jewelled cellophane. Each is excruciatingly lovely, but it dissolves quickly as the page turns. Readers, however are not saddened by this ephemeral nature for Ruefle's style is so manifold, every turn summons something new.'
— Valerie Pell, *Third Coast*

Praise for *The Book*

'*The Book* explores the bittersweetness of getting older.... In a whirlwind of people and places, Vermont's solitude-loving poet laureate paints a picture of a life lived in the company of many others.'
— Donna Vatnick, *The Los Angeles Review*

'Ruefle has excelled in writing agile, syncopated free verse, but her prose poems are even more unusual. Her investigations in the genre have yielded a sound all her own. You hear in these new poems how poetic prose can absorb and parody the regular prose of daily life: articles, advertisements, letters to the editor, legal documents, business correspondence.'
— Jim Schley, author of *As When, In Season*

'The potent pieces resist easy interpretation, sparkling with the suggestiveness of Ruefle's poetry. Readers will marvel at the results.'
— *Publishers Weekly*

Praise for *My Private Property*

'This is a book you want to read slowly, to savour both for what it says and how Ruefle says it. And even more remarkable is the way she lures you, the reader, in, and gets you to suspend your disbelief. I do not know of another book like *My Private Property*.'
— John Yau, *Hyperallergic*

'Ruefle can seem like a supernally well-read person who has grown bored with what smartness looks like, and has grown attracted to the other side.... She is not writing with a prescription, or at least not one for this earth. Nor is she celebrating the commonplace. She is concentrating on one thing at a time and doing something that, depending on how the light strikes it, can look like weirding out or being very serious.'
— *New York Times*

'The property that Ruefle deems private is the impalpable nature of the inner life we all share; it is at once ours and everyone's.... Ruefle has shown a talent for elevating her acute observations and narrative inclination well above mere anecdote to create quietly disquieting moments – a literature of barbed ambiguity and unresolved disruption.'
— *Bookforum*

'In *My Private Property*, all of life can be mined for meaning – the pieces concern themselves with the small and the large without making value distinctions between the two. Ruefle deals as frequently with mundane matters – a Christmas tree, feeding a finch, crumbs on a kitchen counter – as with those capital-letter concepts: God, Love, Death, Time, Memory. Any of these "other things" can undergo some transubstantiation and become poetry.'
— *Los Angeles Review of Books*

Fitzcarraldo Editions

—

THE BOOK

EDITOR'S NOTE

Mary Ruefle is an impishly impossible writer to categorize. In the three collections that make up *Golden Crumbs*, as with all her work, we read multiplicities: we have the philosophical intrigue of a stretched aphorism, the taut economy of the prose poem, the surrealism of a wildly plotted short story. Narrative, language, form: all markers of a text are infused with an elegant effervescence, a straight-faced approach to the absurd, a pictorial approach to the story. The reader is never sure-footed in the undulating rhythms of Ruefle's adept style.

To publish three of Ruefle's early prose is to consider her gargantuan influence; her tone and mode are an inspiration for the many writers who follow her. When editing this book, we had a decision to make – a selected prose, or to publish the collections as they appeared in their entirety in 2008, 2013 and 2017. We chose to publish each collection in their full iteration, struck by the discovery of how they spoke to each other, breaching their moments in time. The new proximity between *The Most of It*, *My Private Property* and *The Book* brings Ruefle's connections and accumulations together in bombastic, puzzling, energized joy. *Golden Crumbs* creates new stories from these three books singing together and in succession.

Rachael Allen, London, July 2026

THE MOST OF IT

To you

"Hardly had we entered the cemetery when we lost one another. The trees that had pushed up between the graves blocked our view, and our shouts went unanswered. And then, just as suddenly, we found one another again..."
— Tzvetan Todorov

SNOW

Every time it starts to snow, I would like to have sex. No matter if it is snowing lightly and unseriously, or snowing very seriously, well on into the night, I would like to stop whatever manifestation of life I am engaged in and have sex, with the same person, who also sees the snow and heeds it, who might have to leave an office or meeting, or some arduous physical task, or, conceivably, leave off having sex with another person, and go in the snow to me, who is already, in the snow, beginning to have sex in my snow-mind. Someone for whom, like me, this is an ultimatum, the snow sign, an ultimatum of joy, though as an ultimatum beyond joy as well as sorrow. I would like to be in the classroom—for I am a teacher—and closing my book stand up, saying "It is snowing and I must go have sex, goodbye," and walk out of the room. And starting my car, in the beginning stages of snow, know that he is starting his car, with the flakes falling on its windshield, or, if he is at home, he is looking at the snow and knowing I will arrive, snowy, in ten or twenty or thirty minutes, and, if the snow has stopped off, we, as humans, can make a decision, but not while it is still snowing, and even half-snow would be something to be obeyed. I often wonder where the birds go in a snowstorm, for they disappear completely. I always think of them deep inside the bushes, and further along inside the trees and deep inside of the forests, on branches where no snow can reach, deeply recessed for the time of the snow, not oblivious to it, but intensely accepting their incapacity, and so enduring the snow in brave little inborn ways, with their feathered heads bowed down for warmth. Wings, the mark of a bird, are quite useless in snow. When I am inside having sex while it snows I want to be thinking about the birds too, and I want my love to love thinking about the birds as much as I do, for it is snowing and we are having sex under or on top of the blankets and the birds cannot be that far away, deep in the stillness and silence of the snow, their breasts still have color, their hearts are beating, they breathe in and out while it snows all around them, though thinking about the birds is not as fascinating as watching it snow on a cemetery, on graves and tombstones and the vaults of the dead, I love watching it snow on graves, how cold the snow is, even colder the stones, and the ground is the coldest of all, and the bones of the dead are in the ground, but the dead are not cold, snow or no snow, it means very little to them, nothing, it means nothing to them, but for us, watching it snow on the dead, watching the graveyard get covered in snow, it is very cold, the snow on top of the graves over the bones, it seems especially cold, and at the same time especially peaceful, it is like snow falling gently on sleepers, even if it falls in a hurry it seems gentle, because the sleepers are gentle, they are not anxious, they are sleeping through the snow and they will be sleeping beyond the snow, and although I will be having sex while it snows I want to remember the quiet, cold, gentle sleepers who cannot think of themselves as birds nestled in feathers, but who are themselves, in part, part of the snow, which is falling with such steadfast devotion to the ground all the anxiety in the world seems gone, the world seems deep in a bed as I am deep in a bed, lost in the arms of my lover, yes, when it snows like this I feel the whole world has joined me in isolation and silence.

CAMP WILLIAM

This morning I want to talk a little bit about killing. You know it is never easy. There can never be enough killing. It is the biggest earthly part of time yet we are often shy of it. What a slow, discouraging business it can seem. It's fight, fight, fight and then some, with hardly a sign of encouragement to keep you going. But each of us must try. When we are young we are anxious to grow up and start killing but as soon as we are older we grasp the full measure of how difficult it really is. The secrets of the dark struggles of the night are well concealed. When I was a child my father often took me with him to visit various military installations, and to enter each one we had first to pass through a little gate where a guard waved at us and we were expected to wave back. It was of course really a salute, but really it looks something like a little wave, it *is* a little wave, and I was struck, as a child, by the fact two strangers—my father and the guard, who most certainly did not know each other—were expressing such open and friendly affection for each other. This wonderful feeling has never left me, and in many ways has led me to standing here before you today. If two strangers can express such unspoken goodwill toward each other, how much more so must take place when we are killing! For the greatest acts of killing take place between strangers, strangers for whom there exists this wonderful capacity for intimate connection. Think of it! Somewhere there exists a stranger waiting for you to kill him in such an honest and heartrending way. Or perhaps he will kill you, so glorious and inexplicable is life. I actually tremble when I speak of these things, for I know your hearts are good at the core, and that you are deserving of all life has to offer, and that one day your courage will burst its very vessels. Well, I will not keep you from your canoes any longer. But today when you are out rowing upon the waters, I hope each of you will take a moment to consider the strength you possess in your own two arms.

SUBURB OF LONG SUFFERING

Fire is my companion, but I do not talk to it, it talks to me. It has white-hot fissures that quiver and rage and complain and sometimes very tender speech towards morning, a low blue word or two. I never tire of listening to my fire. Music is my companion also, but it does not talk to me, I talk to it, I talk to it and it listens without complaint, absorbing whatever I am feeling and I can feel it listening to me. I think it never tires of listening to me. Together, the fire and the music and me, we make a family that, despite its dysfunction, is able to persevere. Yet I have a complaint. When they are in the room together, the fire and the music, they talk to each other and neither do they talk nor listen to me, as for example on a rainy day when the three of us come into the room together to while away the time: the fire and the music begin to converse in soft tones at first, so as not to disturb me I like to think, but soon their conversation grows to such a pitch that between the two of them there seem to be a great many unspoken agreements, while I am left feeling lonelier and lonelier, and end up by the window, a mere eavesdropper in my own home.

MY PET, MY CLOCK

A pet is a good way to tell time, better than a clock, for time is a measure of the changing positions of objects, and soon it will be time to feed the pet, to exercise the pet, to replace its little ball, clip its nails or talons, wash it ever so gently, vacuum up its sheddings and so forth. And eventually the sad day comes when it must die, and then it is time to get another. A clock, on the other hand and against all appearances, is a very poor way to tell time, for all it ever does is sit there or hang on the wall, and very seldom does it do anything of itself to remind you of time. Of course we live in a country where twice a year time springs forward or falls back, and on those occasions—the mock birthdays of time—a little fuss must be made over the clock, but other than that it does not really ask for much. If you are desirous of saving time one of the best things you can do is buy your clock batteries on one of its birthdays, eliminating the need for a gift on the next occasion. But other than these few inconveniences the care of your clock will never be a way of marking time, despite the fact we bring them into our homes for just this purpose. A clock is in fact no better than a dead pet. I myself have neither clock nor pet, and well might you ask what I do for time, though I prefer to put it somewhat differently: what has time ever done for me? Very little, it would seem; time has robbed me of my youth, my energy, strength, sprite, the vigor I was in my childhood famous for, and all the natural oils in my once-luxurious tresses. Once I felt enough for time to invest in a little goldfish, but alas he died two days later in a gallant attempt to jump his bowl, which was successful, though not in time, for in England there is a physicist by the name of Julian

Barbour who believes time does not exist as we commonly perceive it to exist, that is in a passing continuum; no, he believes time, our time, time on earth, is made up of unconnected, absolutely discrete units, the length of an instant, which eternally occur, having no past and no future. In this sense of time, my goldfish is forever happily swimming in his new bowl and forever leaping from it in an adventurous frolic, or spasm of despair, depending on your view, which is also subject to time, as it is evident the views of old age do not coincide with youthful ones. But in this other world, the world of discrete eternal units, your pet needs his dinner, as he is whining at his bowl, yet does not need his dinner, as he has just eaten and is lying by the fire. Your pet has become a most inaccurate way of marking time, whereas the lifeless clock on the mantle, a discrete unit itself, dependent on no one and subject not to the passing of time, will finally have its day and serve its true purpose of marking time, which neither moves forward nor falls back, requiring no adjustments whatsoever, though, when this day comes and the clock is restored to its rightful place in our homes, if not our hearts, I often wonder if it will still be said when looking at a clock, as is the custom now, *how beautiful it is to have lived, how blessed that one can die*.

HAZELINE

After father died, he said that dying had taken a longer time than he had previously imagined possible. He was not dead at that time but we did not know it, his eyes had long ceased being the source of anything, he was stiff as a board and he had no pulse. Mother and I were very interested in everything he had to say, the way the living are with experts. He said it was extremely painful, even now, but not in any way that he could explain or describe. Speaking was painful, he said, more painful than anything else, because being dead—he couldn't describe it—it didn't amount to very much, there was no way we could understand, and by the time we ourselves died he would be long gone. He said there was a woman down the hall who was also dead, though no one knew it yet, and he could talk to her, but she wasn't listening. Mother bristled when he said this, and I put my hand on her arm. He was telling about how people when they are dead know each other by little signs that are not of this world when Doctor Fillmore came in and said Dad would be fine, though he didn't use those words exactly, he used "the old board with iron nails in it is an otter again." That was Dad. It didn't take anyone long to get to know him, a lot less time than it took to die, according to him who died six hours or days or weeks later, we could not be sure, as he had always been fond of making us feel we were floating away while he was standing on the coast of Iceland singing.

LICHEN

I wanted to go into the forest and collect lichen. I wanted to use the lichen in an art project because it had a crumbly, scaly texture and various shades of the same color appeared in the smallest patches. I was pretty sure lichen was rootless, but whether its living would be interrupted or unsettled in some way I was unsure. I didn't want to pick lichen if picking it in any way resembled kidnapping. I seemed to recall lichen was very old, among the oldest living things on earth, and that deserved considerable respect, but at the same time there had to be young lichen, if lichen was living it had to reproduce fairly regularly and so some of the lichen had to be young. I did not know how to tell young lichen from old lichen, I did not know if young lichen and old lichen lived together, I did not know which of them, the old or the young, was better suited to kidnapping, I thought it true in general that the older the living thing the closer it was to the end of its life cycle and the less harm there was in kidnapping it, but also true in general that the younger a thing, the less its grip was on its own life—in this case the rock or bark—and the more willing it would be to be lifted out of its environment, I mean the easier it would be to take. If the old lichen clung most tenaciously to its rock or bark, it would be more difficult to do the "right" thing, and if the young lichen could be fairly coaxed off the rock or bark, the easier it would be to do the "wrong" thing. I sat and had these thoughts before I put on my coat to go into the forest and collect my lichen. "My" lichen—it seemed already to be in my possession. To eliminate as much confusion as possible I decided I would collect only dead lichen. I knew that lichen was not of my species and certainly did not bury their dead; therefore the dead lichen must be everywhere in the forest, among the living, among the very old lichen and among the young lichen, and I would find them. But how? How could I recognize the dead lichen among the living lichen? Surely the dead lichen did not perceptively move, but nor did the living lichen perceptively move. I had to admit I could not tell the difference between the living and the dead. Such an incapacity shocked me. If that were my criteria it would be easier to collect bears, though, of course, in other ways, more difficult, and as I went out the door I understood, with some certainty I think, why bears are often on the minds of those who brave the forest.

A GLASS OF WATER

I needed to open the refrigerator—the water I wanted was there, sitting inside a glass pitcher on the uppermost grill, cold and clear and perfectly suited to my thirst. But I was afraid of the light, the light that went on whenever I opened the door, or the light that was always on—it was hard to tell—and I was more afraid of the light than I wanted the water. Still, my desire for the water was so strong I sometimes put my hand on the door, preparing, in my mind, to open the door more quickly than the light could respond to the door being opened, and sometimes I tried a completely spontaneous approach, believing if I opened the door *very* quickly, without thinking of either the water or the light, and most of all without thinking of opening the door (while I was opening it), I might be able to overcome the light, my fear, like most fear, being predicated on premeditation, but when this didn't work I entertained the very reasonable idea of waiting until the source of the light—the lightbulb—burned itself out, as was inevitable, though how this could happen if I didn't open the door once in all those years was a problem, compounded by the very real possibility of my dying of thirst while I waited. To use the light again and again seemed to be my only recourse if I wanted to burn the light out, and as it happened I opened the door again and again, but now I was more intent on the light than I was on the water, and forgot to drink altogether as I stood in the kitchen in my stocking feet in front of the refrigerator, opening and closing the door in rapid succession, driven by dehydration and fear to take risks that led me deeper and deeper into crisis.

WOMAN WITH A YELLOW SCARF

I was reading in bed in the morning, something I like to do, something I try to do every thirty days, two or three hours, usually on a Sunday. Reading in bed in the morning is not like reading at any other hour—first thing!—your mind fresh and alive and responsive, sometimes you read something you would miss at any other hour, especially the late ones, midnight, that's another time for reading and there are things you don't miss at midnight but they are not the things you don't miss in the morning. That was when I saw her. *A woman passed holding a yellow scarf over her head.* She does this in a story by Albert Camus. A French engineer is in a remote village in Brazil, the mayor has given him lodgings in the hospital, which is called by the curious name of "Happy Memory," which is not so curious when you consider the building of a hospital in a village that has none is a happy memory for those who live there and will use it. Our protagonist wakes up in Happy Memory hospital, it's raining, he looks out the window at a clump of aloes being rained on, and then the sentence happens. *A woman passed holding a yellow scarf over her head.* A simple sentence, of no import in the story—our lady never again appears, and without her presence on page 169 (in my copy) the story would not appear to be missing a single necessary moment. Yet the yellow scarf is needed by this woman at this moment, it is raining, she is passing by the hospital, she doesn't want to get her hair wet, or her head, or her body, luckily she has a yellow scarf she can hold over her head, stretched like a sail between two hands, or maybe not, maybe the scarf is triangulated and she is holding it under her chin. Who is she? Where is she on her way to, or coming from, how old is she, is she married with children or not? What difference can it make, this fictional woman is born and dies in the same sentence, her moment passes us holding its yellow scarf, her fate is to appear in a story by Camus, and when I think of her fate I realize it could be worse, she could be walking past a window in a story by Thomas Gilbert, surely a woman can sense the importance of whose story she is in, perhaps that is why she chose, this morning, to bring along her yellow scarf—a keen author couldn't fail to notice that. Still, her fate cannot be commended, one day it is raining, she puts on a yellow scarf and goes out in the rain, never to be heard from or seen again. She is among the missing, but we don't even know her name, or what she looks like. I doubt the scarf was made of silk, canary yellow with a map of the world on it. I have such a scarf draped over a wooden hanger in my coat closet, I have had it many years and never once worn it, rain or no rain, I do not recall how I came by it, perhaps it was given to me. But in this remote village in Brazil in the nineteen hundred and fifties, this yellow scarf—well, maybe, ok, silk. I often fall into the habit of thinking anyone born in the ages before I was born lived in the dark ages. Nothing could be further from the truth, as they say, but I've noticed people everywhere stand as far from the truth as possible. *A woman passed holding a yellow scarf over her head.* I don't remember half the scarves or half the women I see in an ordinary day. But this woman was different. She held her head up high as she walked across the street in the rain, and I came to believe she was on a mysterious and important errand, whose nature I might never know, and that somewhere concealed on her body she was carrying the tip of a forefinger wrapped in a bit of yellow fur inside a white leather ring box, and that the finger was mine, I had used it to follow words, for words seemed to me to be always walking alone at night, even in broad daylight they were walking alone at midnight, and I confess, yes, I shadowed them, I shadowed them by way of the alley that is always there and always empty and narrow and hopeless and yields not a single clue.

THE BENCH

My husband and I were arguing about a bench we wanted to buy and put in part of our backyard, a part which is actually a meadow of sorts, a half-acre with tall grasses and weeds and the occasional wildflower because we do not mow it but leave it scrubby and unkempt. This bench would hardly ever be used and in the summer when the grasses were high would remain partially hidden from view. We both knew we wanted the bench to be made of teak so that it would last a long time in the harsh weather and so that we would never have to paint it. Teak weathers to a soft silver that might, in November or March, disappear into the gray hills that are the backdrop of our lives. My husband wanted a four-foot bench and I wanted a five-foot bench. This is what we argued about. My husband insisted that a four-foot bench was all we needed, since no more than two people (presumably ourselves) would ever sit on it at the same time. I felt his reasoning was not only beside the point but missed it entirely; I said what mattered most to me was the idea of the bench, the look of it there, to be gazed at with only the vaguest notion it could hold more people than would ever actually sit down. The life of the bench in my imagination was more important than any practical function the bench might serve. After all, I argued, we wanted a bench so that we could look at it, so that we could imagine sitting on it, so that, unexpectedly, a bird might sit on it, or fallen leaves, or inches of snow, and the longer the bench, the greater the expanse of that plank, the more it matched its true function, which was imaginary. My husband mentioned money and I said that I was happier to have no bench at all, which would cost nothing, than to have a four-foot bench, which would be expensive. I said that having no bench at all was closer to the five-foot bench than the four-foot bench because having no bench served the imagination in similar ways, and so not having a bench became an option in our argument, became a third bench. We grew very tired of discussing the three benches and for a day we rested from our argument. During this day I had many things to do and many of them involved my driving past other houses, none of which had benches, that is they each had the third bench, and as I drove past the other houses I could see a bench here and a bench there; sometimes I saw the bench very close to the house, against a wall or on a porch, and sometimes I saw the bench under a tree or in the open grass, cut or uncut, and once I saw the bench at the end of the driveway, blocking the road. Always it was a five-foot bench that I saw, a long sleek bench or a broken-down bench, a bench with a slatted back or a bench with a solid, carved back, and always the bench was empty. But I knew that for my husband the third bench was only four feet long and he saw always two people sitting on it, two happy or tired people, two people who were happy to be alive or two people tired from having worked hard enough to buy the bench they were sitting on. Or they were happy and tired, happy to have reached the end of some argument, tired from having had it. For these people, the bench was an emblem of their days, which were fruitful because their suffering had come to an end. On my bench, which was always empty, nothing had come to an end because nothing had begun, no one had sat down, though the bench was always there waiting for exactly that to happen. And the bench was always long enough so that someone, if he desired to, could lie all the way down. That day passed. Another day followed it and my husband and I began, once more, to discuss the bench. The sound of our voices revealed a renewed interest and vigor. I thought I sensed in him a coming around to my view of the bench and I know he sensed in me a coming around to his view of the bench, because at one point I said that a four-foot bench reminded me of rough notes towards a real bench while a five-foot bench was like a fragment of an even longer bench and I admitted it was at times hard to tell the difference. He said he didn't know anything about the difference between rough notes and fragments but he agreed that between the two benches there was, possibly, just perhaps—he could imagine it—very little difference. It was, after all, only a foot we were talking about. And I think it was then, in both of our minds, that a fourth bench came into being, a bench that was only a foot long, a miniature bench, a bench we could build ourselves, though of course we did not. This seemed to be, essentially, the bench we were talking about. Much later, when the birds came back, or the leaves drifted downwards, or the snow fell, slowly and lightly at first, then heavier and faster, it was this bench that we both saw when we looked out the window at the bench we eventually placed in the meadow which continued to grow as if there were no bench at all.

MONUMENT

A small war had ended. Like all wars, it was terrible. Things which had stood in existence were now vanished. I had come back because I had survived and survivors come back, there is nothing else left for them to do. I had been on long travels connected to the war, and I had been to the centerpiece of the war, that acre of conflagration. And now I was sitting on a park bench, watching ducks land and take off from a pond. They too had survived, though I had no way of knowing if they were the same ducks from before the war or if they were the offspring of ducks who had died in the war. It was a warm day in the capital and people were walking without coats, dazed by the warmth, which was not the heat of war, which had engulfed them, but the warmth of expansion, in which would grow the idea of a memorial to the war, which had ended, and of which I was a veteran architect. I knew I would be called upon for my ideas in regards to this memorial and I had entered the park aimlessly, trying to escape my ideas, as I had been to the centerpiece, that acre of conflagration, and from there the only skill that returned was escapement, any others died with those who possessed them. I was dining with friends that evening, for the restaurants and theaters and shops had reopened, the capital was like a great tablecloth being shaken in mid-air so that life could be smoothed and reset and go on, and I had in my mind a longing to eat, and to afterwards order my favorite dessert, cherries jubilee, which would be made to flame and set in the center of the table, and I had in my mind the idea of submitting to the committee a drawing of an enormous plate of cherries, perpetually burning, to be set in the center of the park, as a memorial to the war, that acre of conflagration. And perhaps also in my mind was the hope that such a ridiculous idea would of course be ignored and as a result I would be left in peace, the one thing I desired, even beyond cherries. And I could see the committee, after abandoning my idea, remaining in their seats fighting over the designs of others, far into the after hours of the work day, their struggles never seeming to end, and then I wanted to submit an idea of themselves as a memorial for the war, the conference table on an island in the middle of the pond, though at least some of them would have to be willing to be cast in agony. And then I saw on the ground an unnamed insect in its solitary existence, making its laborious way through tough blades of grass that threatened its route, and using a stick that lay nearby I drew a circle around the animal—if you can call him that—and at once what had been but a moment of middling drama became a theater of conflict, for as the insect continued to fumble lop-sided in circles it seemed to me that his efforts had increased, not only by my interest in them, but by the addition of a perimeter which he now seemed intent on escaping. I looked up then, and what happened next I cannot describe without a considerable loss of words: I saw a drinking fountain. It had not suddenly appeared, it must have always been there, it must have been there as I walked past it and sat down on the bench, it must have been there yesterday, and during the war, and in the afternoons before the war. It was a plain gunmetal drinking fountain, of the old sort, a basin on a pedestal, and it stood there, an ordinary object that had become an unspeakable gift, a wonder of civilization, and I had an overwhelming desire to see if it worked, I stood up then and approached it timidly, as I would a woman, I bent low and put my hand on its handle and my mouth hovered over its spigot—I wanted to kiss it, I was going to kiss it—and I remembered with a horrible shock that in rising from the bench I had stepped on and killed the insect, I could hear again his death under my left foot, though this did not deter me from finishing my kiss, and as the water came forth with a low bubbling at first and finally an arch that reached my mouth, I began to devise a secret route out of the park that would keep me occupied for some time, then I looked up, holding the miraculous water in my mouth, and saw the ducks in mid-flight, their wings shedding water drops which returned to the pond, and remembered in amazement that I could swallow, and I did, then a bit of arcane knowledge returned to me from an idle moment of reading spent years ago, before the war: that a speculum is not only an instrument regarded by most with horror, as well as an ancient mirror, and a medieval compendium of all knowledge, but a patch of color on the lower wing segments of most ducks and some other birds. Thus I was able, in serenest peace, to make my way back to my garret and design the memorial which was not elected and never built, but remained for me an end to the war that had ended.

BEAUTIFUL DAY

I was walking to the post office when I happened to pass R—, a slight acquaintance on account of our having the same last name, as was discovered one year–oh, many years ago–at the voting poll. We were standing in line next to one another and I remember our conversation vividly. Actually we did not speak to one another, but when you are standing in line next to a man who precedes you into a narrow booth with a thick curtain hung on rings over a pole, and he is lost from view for a full five minutes which must be a terror for him as it will be for you, who can never remember the many names of the remarkable persons running for office, to the extent that on the previous evening I had written them in ballpoint on the palm of my hand, which was now sweating to the degree they had become illegible–well, as I insinuated, though we said nothing, how could we forget one another, thrown into circumstances like that? R— came out of the booth, a volunteer called my name, and I think not a person in the room, which was overflowing with people, failed to note a person of one name preceded a person of the same name, or at the very least a person of one name following a person with the same name. Since our introduction then, almost nothing–an occasional nod, a nod of the head, yes, but a nod that is at once personal and touching, a charming, open, benevolent nod, this we sometimes exchanged, sometimes he initiated the nod and sometimes it was I, but I am a shy person, as is, I believe, constantly observed by those who live in this town. I was walking to the post office, I had walked all the way in fact and was now standing in front of it, when R— said quite distinctly–I do not think I was imagining it–*hello*. I do not think a nod preceded this unexpected and curious addition to our relationship but I was shocked by its intimacy to the degree that I do not remember if a nod preceded it. Perhaps a nod came after? I cannot recall. Taking great care not to lose control over my faculties altogether I said to R—: *hello*. This word, following so soon after the first, stunned me with the power of communication possible between two souls who have heretofore labored so intently to keep their human capacity for passion latent. At that moment I realized it was a beautiful day–indeed it was a very beautiful day, overabundant, radiant in all aspects of itself, the flag flying like a certificate of rapturous appreciation for the clouds, which were sailing directly overhead across a clear blue sky, and in the window boxes attached to the brick facade of the building pert crocuses stood in a bright array, it seemed to me they were like responsive ears, alert to whatever R— or I might venture to say next; perhaps it was on account of this fantasy that I hesitated, I hesitated to speak what I felt and say what I knew to be true: *it is a beautiful day*. But would such a confession, I asked myself in my hesitation, be too prompt, too rash, coming so soon after the two *hellos*, which had already fallen in such rapid progression that R— might, like myself, be quaking from an inability to keep up with all that had already happened? Might R— feel I was pushing the day forward at an alarming and unjust rate, even if part of its undeniable beauty was that very quickening? These thoughts and more like them prevented the spontaneous expression I should have liked so much to make before R— was gone. R— did not hesitate, that is for certain– he sailed like a cloud into the post office, nod or no nod (why wasn't I paying *more attention*?) and I was stuck fast by the crocuses, the flag unfurled over us all, when the decision came over me to begin my way home, immediately and with brio, that I might lose no further step with the day, which was beautiful, and with the future which had shown itself to be quick but kind, allowing me these little moments to catch up with it, and keep pace with it when I could.

AUG 19 It took the little birds—are they wrens?—about a week to find the seeds.

AUG 23 One day a pigeon joined them, he was larger and seemed "superior," the wrens seemed "respectful," as if they were deferring to him.

(later) I saw a bird in the bushes near Dairy Queen. It looked thin to me.

(later) There were about ten little wrens at work on the seed when someone on the street revved up a motorcycle—nine of the wrens instantly flew to the nearest tree, all together, but one little wren did not—he just stayed and kept on eating.
a) was he smarter than the others?
b) was he dumber than the others?
c) was he simply deaf?

A minute later all the wrens in the tree flew off together and when the wren who stayed behind to work on the seed *saw* them (with his eyes) he instantly joined them—he didn't want to be left behind! But when they were just going to the tree he hadn't minded one bit.

AUG 24 A hawk circling very high up in the heavens.

AUG 25 Some of the birds have told me their names; the rest are so far quiet.

(later) I dare not log the amount of time I spend sitting

on the ledge of the kitchen window, watching the wrens on the flat black asphalt roof where I have placed a red frisbee of water and a blue frisbee of seed.

AUG 26 They come for breakfast and they come for dinner. WHERE DO THEY GO FOR LUNCH?

AUG 28 Bought a pair of opera glasses to facilitate my search among the birds.

AUG 29 I replace the little golden seeds, for I have run out of them, with black oiled sunflower seeds, which everyone knows are superior and preferred by all birds. I do this in the middle of the night so as to "surprise" the birds in the morning. But in the morning they don't act "surprised" at all, they act as if nothing's changed. But then again, they may be "acting."

(later) They ARE acting—the wrens don't like the new seed, they are ignoring it! Do they KNOW how much work it took to lug that bag up the stairs?

AUG 30 Now the pigeon comes around and does a terrible thing, an inexplicable thing—he scatters all the seed by standing in the frisbee and with his head down in the seed swings his head from side to side, not eating but *sweeping* the seeds out of the frisbee and onto the roof, all over the roof; he seems angry, as if he's searching for something he can't find.

(later) The truth is, none of us really feed the birds because we care for them; we feed them because we like to watch.

(later) But was the PIGEON caring for the birds? Was the big bird caring for the little birds? Because now that the big seeds are SCATTERED, all the little wrens come and eat them joyfully off the roof.

SEPT 1 Early this morning a cardinal appears out of nowhere, looking like Santa Claus.

(later) Suddenly it occurs to me this just might be the birds' Christmas—I must do something quick, something special.

(later) Went out and bought six paper bags of French fries, carefully arranging them in the frisbee so their ends were up.

(later) A dove comes, a pale gray soft dove, smaller than the pigeons but larger than the wrens. Doves are lovebirds, how can they come in anything less than a pair? My medium dove must be a heartbroken one.

My French fries are eaten by the medium heartbroken dove.

Is there anything sadder than the sight of a medium heartbroken dove stuffed with French fries on Christmas morning?

SEPT 2 Is there anything better, more beautiful, in all the world, across all the lands, over the Taj Mahal and everything, than two pigeons, ten wrens, a cardinal, and a medium heartbroken dove come to Ohio, to an asphalt roof, to eat potatoes on the day AFTER Christmas?

(later) A piece of available sky.

SEPT 3 Wrens are described as having "upturned tail feathers," that being their DISTINGUISHING feature, and my little browny-gray birds do NOT—mine have flat, outgoing tails like musical reeds.

(later) Is it that we can never name that which we love?

SEPT 4 I would look it up in a book, but it is a sin to look up that which you love in a book.

SEPT 9 Most beautiful blackbird I've ever seen—sleek, all sheen, positively indigo head/throat, wearing a turquoise necklace on top of that!

SEPT 10 Susan says the little wren-who-is-not-a-wren, the one who stayed to gorge while the others fled, was displaying "desperate gluttony," a condition in which he repressed his deeper, more constant, tragic terror, out of which arose indomitable seed greediness, a mere symptom of deeper hungers. I think this means he stayed because he was MORE terrified than the others, not less.

SEPT 11 One pigeon (rock dove!) is magnificently all brown in the body, but his tail is white. He looks like a horse.

SEPT 12 On December 9, 1531, the neophyte Juan Diego was lured to Mount Tepeyac by the sound of stunning music. He made his way to the top and the Virgin of Guadalupe appeared to him in radiant splendor. Could it have been a thrush?

SEPT 13 This morning all the little gray-brown no-names looked fuzzier than usual—I thought they were baby chicks toddling in a barnyard.

SEPT 14 The Bible says we are living through the greatest mass-extinction period in the planet's history.

SEPT 15 When I buy my weekly bag of seeds at Ace Hardware, a 25-lb bag for eight dollars and some cents, the man I buy them from carries the bag out to my car for me, and I thank him. This doesn't seem worth noting, except whenever it happens I have the distinct impression we are being watched.

SEPT 17 I don't know what has happened, but all my little gray-browns have disappeared and a similar number of VERY PLUMP gray-browns have taken their place! Lined up on the telephone wire—which overhangs the roof—they look like a bunch of beer bottles, or a line of tits, which is the same thing.

SEPT 18 Although all poets aspire to be birds, no bird aspires to be a poet.

SEPT 19 If I don't feed them for a single day, they stop coming! And I look back over my life, to an autumn day years and years ago, when my (then) therapist told me there are very few things one can take personally; apparently I am still struggling with this.

SEPT 20 Some days just to tell a bird from a tree is asking a lot.

SEPT 21 Though this country was founded on principles

of freedom, nowhere in the United States Constitution do they mention birds.

SEPT 22 Kate and Pete keep frozen yellow finches in their freezer, in zip-lock bags, for the purposes of "drawing and photography."

SEPT 23 I lost my long brown wallet, and in it were my credit card, my debit card, my checkbook, my checkbook register, my video club card, my Osco card, my Grand Union card, my Co-op card, my oil-change card, my automobile club card, my driver's license, my medical insurance card, my cash, my change, my slips and bits of paper with the names of books, films, and musical recordings I want to experience before I die, the names and numbers of human beings I could call if I were ever in an emergency or lost or sad, and when I lost my long brown wallet with all this stuff in it, I felt like a bird, and it was wonderful.

SEPT 24 Eating dinner on the window ledge, I am watching my birds as I gnaw on a chicken thigh. There I am, chewing my dead bird in front of living birds. As soon as I realize this, I am ashamed, and keep on eating.

SEPT 25 What if half the people you knew, and half the people you loved, were dead within a year? Last night on the phone Ralph was so depressed I didn't know what to do, so I said, out of the blue, "Do you want to talk about the avian flu?"

(later) Sorrow thy name is sparrow.

SEPT 27 With folded wings.

SEPT 28 No more prayers. Say instead, as many times as you can, the word SPARROW. Soon you will be saying O SPARE O SPARE O SPARE O SPARE.

SEPT 29 In the palm of the child's hand is a bird.

THE DART AND THE DRILL

I do not believe that when my brother pierced my skull with a succession of darts thrown from across our paneled rec room on the night of November 18th in my sixth year on earth, he was trying to transcend the notions of time and space as contained and protected by the human skull. But who can fathom the complexities of the human brain? Ten years later—this would have been in 1967—*The New York Times* reported a twenty-four-year-old man, who held an honors degree in law, died in the process of using a dentist's drill on his own skull, positioned an inch above his right ear, in an attempt to prove that time and space could be conquered. He had taken a tab of acid an hour earlier and, in a state of expanded—some might say exaggerated—consciousness, hit upon this singular proof. Ever since my brother darted me I have lived in a state of expanding consciousness—mine grew and grew until they called me old—but not once have I taken a drill to myself. I have considered a gun. I have worn hats. I have had a magnificent hairdresser. The art of trepanning—surgically cutting out discs of bone from the skull using a trephine—derives from the art of mining rock by using a similar tool for sinking shafts; who has not wondered what it would be like to journey to the center of the earth, and who has not coveted what valuables can be picked up on the way down? Necklaces and bracelets and rings bear witness to our desire to imitate the young man and his conquering drill—to seek, to mine, to plunder, to uncover what is buried deep beneath some surface. My mother always wore a gold linked bracelet because it was given to her by a boy she fancied before she met my father. This boy wanted to know my mother, but how far he got in their ice-cream soda conversations is not known to me, it being safe to say my father got further in *his* late-night conversations, trepanning her mind with a nonchalance and skill I can only imagine, trepanning her mind for another fifty years, at which point he gave her his own gold tooth hanging from a chain, about which she had very little to say, and said it by never wearing it. The human brain seems to be obsessed with boring into other brains, and if none are available, one's own brain will do quite well, if one is smart enough to see that mysteries lie within as well as without, and you would be surprised, actually, to know how few are left on earth who seriously consider themselves worth investigating, and, sadly, our young man with a drill is no longer among them. Astronauts and mechanical rovers always dig a little when they reach another planet, while there is a shaft in the desert here that never stops hauling, and certain mines have been in continuous operation for centuries. Across time, across space, the ruby and emerald-throated hummingbirds fly, with their exquisitely long beaks working nonstop to dart the flowers. There is that, O my brother, and in the summer of love one young human, high on life itself, plugged in an electric drill to see what he would find. What is more, regardless of how he tried to settle these matters, no one has ever stopped trying, no one has ever stopped and said *Enough*, all these things do is make us shudder.

THE TAKING OF MOUNDVILLE BY ZOOM

If you were very, very small, smaller than a leprechaun, smaller than a gnome or a fairy, and you lived in a vagina, every time a penis came in there would be a natural disaster. Your dishes would fall out of the cupboards and break and the furniture slide all the way to the other side of the room. It would take a long time to clean up afterwards.

HARD-BOILED DETECTIVE

If you believe what you have been told, men and women have sex and sex leads to pregnancy and pregnancy produces every known person on the planet. But you have to look beneath the surface. You have to ask questions. How many pregnant women do you actually know? How many pregnant women have you known in your lifetime? If you have known more than twenty you are truly extraordinary. Let's say you are extraordinary. You are a gynecologist! You see twenty pregnant women a day! But you see the same twenty pregnant women a day for nine months. There are twelve months in a year. Even if you worked for fifty years, you would only see one thousand pregnant women, and there are *seven billion* people in the world. In any one of the world's teeming cities, today, at this hour, there are millions of people threading in and out of the shops, in offices, ordering from menus. There are people alone in their rooms, dozing, watering plants, talking on telephones. Did you picture any of these people as pregnant? Of course not, because so few actually are. How many times have you yourself been pregnant? Not seven billion times! Granted, if each person on the planet was pregnant only once, that would account for everyone. But that never happens, it can't happen, it's impossible, there are children, there are the elderly, the infertile, the young girls on birth control, the abortions. I live in a town of 20,000 people and only two were born today. I am conducting my investigations at three o'clock in the afternoon, and it is possible many of my town's inhabitants are having sex at this moment, but it is impossible that they are in the majority. Even at midnight, it's a hard case to crack, because although more people are actually having sex at that hour, in today's world not half the sex we are having actually leads to pregnancy. It doesn't add up. You do the math. In summation: How many pregnant women do you actually know? How many pregnant women did you see on the street today? Now look at all the people in the world. Where did they come from? A deep mystery remains unsolved. Perhaps I go too far, but I think it is the fundamental mystery of life.

WHAT WOMAN

If someone asked me to remember my first menses—for what woman can forget it?—I would remember the afternoon in the dressing room off of the ballet studio, where I was one of twelve disciples in pink and black who had just been whipped to a frenzy in front of a mirror by a Russian voice, and the low bench where I sat undoing my toe shoes, unwinding their long ribbons from around my ankles, mysteriously feeling that my unseen toes had been crushed in a new way, a way that ushered in the idea that love could be greater than pain, devotion could withstand the greatest barbarity, and I was one who could bear it. That wad of lamb's wool stuffed in the blunt end of each shoe was indeed blood-soaked, it was wet, it was red, and yet already turning a dark and troubling purple.

ALL MY ROE

The mystery of mysteries was not a thing to be spoken lightly of, night after night we guessed but never asked, it meant that we were on our way to the Earth, a convulsive shudder now and then and one of us would leave, it was the end of slumber, there would be object lessons, butter, sugar, cake and bones, but never the times we talked late into the fire and adored one another the way we were just there, just together, we would never speak of it but it was there, and never again a comrade like that, to open a door and find everything in love, which somehow made us, daylight we never looked at and went by with a run, out of that door we believed came time, we guessed but never asked, possible back after away and over again we did not know, there was never a weeping like ours, a thousand good nights so next to the next we did not have to speak, who we are we don't know, we are heard thoughts we think, there is a mystery in our atmosphere as yet of nothing and I, the uninitiated, the untried, venture to ask the little beggars of the old Earth each to say a word about it, I did every now and then watch some of them come to the edge of a wide water, and pause, one foot in the air, looking with their keen eyes across it, and swim over, one after the other, till they were all out of sight, and I could only guess where they were by the screaming birds above them.

And I knew somewhere deeply recessed, "away from it all," the real with-it-all took place; there, in the undulating mists, a moose eating the dark green mosses was barely seen through the pines, which were repossessed in the animal's eyebrows (do moose have eyebrows?), craggy and overhanging like the mist and the moss, and all around him millions upon millions of other moose lie dead and buried, and no one had ever had a peek of them (though there were glimpses), and in the glare light of the pizza parlor I chose anchovies which I did not like but seemed ancient and suffering, such small animals, and I took the pie home with me and ate it with my mouth gaping, painfully aware I was not a moose and had never been a moose and would never be a moose, but I had loved you in such an eerie and unnatural way.

SLEEP

She wakes in the middle of the night and puts on a robe, goes to the tap, draws a glass of water, stands at the window, and we can speculate she knows she is not the only person on the planet but at this moment she, our insomniac, believes the others, most of the others in this world, are all peacefully sleeping, which is an illusion, it is not night everywhere, just as in daylight she believes in an endless sky, an illusion, outside the sixty-two vertical miles of pale air—an hour's drive—it is in fact night everywhere and at all times, night is night is night out *there*, but that is just another illusion, night depends on day, no day no night, there is no night there then but something else, something dark and endlessly there in a nightish way. Beyond this, what do we know about our insomniac really? We do not know what her thoughts are but we know she is having them because the expression on her face tells us there is a lot going on inside her head, just as we know from the face of a sleeper that he is dreaming, though we know not what his dreams are. And then—it is now three a.m.—someone wakes in Chicago, someone wakes in Omaha, someone wakes in Denver, and in Minneapolis someone wakes, the robe, the tap, the water, the window, the beliefs, the illusions, the faces, the unknown thoughts. She looks out the window at the snow falling gently in the parking lot, falling on the parked cars and the metal dumpster, the street lights are on and illuminate whole shafts of gently falling snow and there is a lone rabbit out there, hopping and then stopping, hopping and stopping in the snow under the light in the middle of the night, this rabbit, out in the world and disappearing into its shadows.

A CERTAIN SWIRL

The classroom was dark, all the desks were empty, and the sentence on the board was frightened to find itself alone. The sentence wanted someone to read it, the sentence thought it was a fine sentence, a noble, thorough sentence, perhaps a sentence of some importance, made of chalk dust, yes, but a sentence that contained within itself a certain swirl not unlike the nebulous heart of the unknown universe, but if no one read it, how could it be sure? Perhaps it was a dull sentence and that was why everyone had left the room and turned out the lights. Night came, and the moon with it. The sentence sat on the board and shone. It was beautiful to look at, but no one read it.

ASCRIBED THIS DAY TO THE AFFIDAVIT

The street cleaner woke us at five a.m.; from those first distant sounds we were awestruck, and when we looked out it seemed the most beautiful apparition in the world. It was big as a parade float and moved just as slowly, a strange glowing thing whose whirring was now upon us. We tiptoed out to the street and commenced to follow it. One of us had the idea to sprinkle cinnamon in its wake and, all being in general agreement, this is what we did. We followed the truck as it made its ablutionary rounds washing the asphalt with those stiff and rotating brushes, while we shuffled and stooped behind, sprinkling the spice. Thus we completed our dawn devotion, and the world was fragrant and clean, though, to the best of our knowledge, none of the sleepers, when they awoke, were aware of the act that had taken place in the dark, and on their behalf.

THE DIARY

My father was a diary farmer and I grew up on a diary farm. Though it was a small farm, tucked in a valley of rolling pasture bordered by high forest, we always had at least a hundred diaries, four journals and a small cache of notebooks for our own personal use. My job, as far back as I can remember, was to look forward to being happy. In the morning before the mist lifted off, before I walked down the dirt road a good three miles to where it joined the paved road that led to the schoolhouse, it was my job to go into the barn and read the diaries. I could only read one or two at most, before setting off for school, but my father was thankful for even that small amount of hope, and my mother never complained so long as my homework was done. I would sit in the straw on the barn floor, the earliest light streaming in through cracks in the wall, like the shaft of light the movie projector made in the darkened town hall on Friday nights, and some of the chaff from the barn floor floating in that light, particles of straw we used to cover the diaries and other stuff, all afloat in a neverending stream of hope as I lay on the floor and read. We gave all our diaries personal names, and though most people think diaries are all alike, my experience of watching them grow from a mere sentence to a full-blown lock-and-key affair taught me that no two diaries are alike and, like us, each diary deserves its own name. There were general traits, yes; it's true that all diaries prefer stillness to commotion, and for the most part are happiest in the shade and not the sun, but it is equally true that some diaries possess a need to be around other diaries, while some like to be by themselves, and some like to be talked to constantly, while others wander off if you so much as say a word. You'd be surprised by Bessie, a diary I raised from birth, who did her best work wearing a scarf. That was Bessie, who was completely unmanageable until the morning I untied my long woolen scarf and wrapped her in it. When my mother, an otherwise long-suffering and compliant woman, heard I had gone to school without my scarf, she went into the barn to try and take the scarf from Bessie; she did not succeed—mother never did identify with the diaries the way I did—but that night bit her lip in front of me and was forever after that after me for my spelling. I think it was not long afterwards the herd began to thin. Small farmers like my father couldn't compete with the commercial franchises that were subsidized by the government in exchange for meeting a homogenized standard of production. I was in high school by then, and watched my father go from a lean, happy man, proud to be a farmer, to an old, disturbed man, oiling his shotgun in the shed. The herd *had* thinned. Gone were the days we delivered door to door. Gone were the journals we actually read (eventually we were reduced to renting our journals each spring to the commercial men who released them among their own diaries in an effort to improve their heads). The notebooks that we had helped birth on our hands and knees, the notebooks that the family raised so that every Easter they could be opened and read aloud at our own planked table, these resisted the changing times as long as they could, but the day came—I was home from college—my father announced we were going into town to buy a notebook, as our last one had died and it wasn't cost-effective to raise even a sentence from scratch. That was a sad meal, our last before mother passed and father had to lease the acreage to the Salisbury crew. And then—and then—at the very end, at the moment our plan was to sell the farm and move father to a home in town where they had books, at the very moment we were reduced to two diaries and a dog, and not a single notebook or journal still belonged to us, two miracles happened. The first was a fast-developing grass roots movement dedicated to the old diary ways, and a group came forward willing to buy our two remaining diaries for a hefty sum. The second was an explosive market for diary runoff—that would be ash—which had been proved to contain enough potassium to feed a city the size of Kansas. Ash was one thing we had plenty of, for the ashes of old diaries, of pages and ribbons and bindings and backs, had been piling up in the nooks and crannies of our dilapidated barn since before I was born. We had enough genuine ash on the farm to feed the nation. And it was then that my father took a renewed interest in the lives of others, and left the farm to me, and it was I who installed the sifting machines, and I who lived to see the ashes of a lifetime rise again in the barn; night and day they rose, and I could always find a moment or two to myself, especially after father passed, a moment when the chaff-filled beams of light brought back those golden afternoons of my youth, when my job was to look forward to being happy, and here I was, all those years later, in the barn, remembering the old days when a diary would get sick and one of us would have to sit up with it all night long, huddled under the blankets and using a flashlight to keep it calm.

THE MOST OF IT

My Aunt Miel, who never married and whom I never met, was eccentric, and the most of it was her handwriting. She was my mother's sister, and lived at a distance, having gotten a job with the Singer Sewing Machine Company which required her to sit in a storefront and sew so everyone could see for themselves each marvelous new electric model. Everyone said she was made for the job, as she was small of stature and tireless. When she wasn't sewing dresses in the window, her gleaming machine the envy of every woman who walked by, and herself, my mother once told me, the envy of every man who walked by, she wrote us long letters, and their arrival on Thursdays attracted neighborhood attention. Aunt Miel's handwriting was so large no one could read it—at least not easily, or in the usual way. My mother had to stand on our tenement roof to read Aunt Miel's letter, which my sister and I would carefully unfold on the street below. When I was six, one of my favorite games was to stand inside of the Os, and then lie down, for they encircled me perfectly from head to toe, and though there was no point to the game, I would wander happily from O to O, sometimes hopping when there were two in a row, as in the word *soon*. My sister preferred the Ts, on top of which she would align herself with her arms spread out and lie there batting her eyelashes at my mother above. Whenever the word *Tom* occurred, my sister and I would lie on our letters side by side, and her hand would be touching my head. Procuring paper had always been a problem for Aunt Miel, especially during the Depression, but as she had a job she was able, whenever she went to the butcher's (my mother said, too, that Miel was famous for her minced pork) to buy whole rolls of his meat-wrapping paper, which she would unroll into longer and longer sheets, then cut with a pair of Singer sewing scissors, pasting together as many sheets as she needed to say what she had to say. It seemed she was incapable of anything less. My mother said when Miel was a little girl, and indeed she never grew up to be very big, Miel and her handwriting were the scourge of the household; from the time she first learned her letters they were gargantuan. On her very first day of school she sat at her desk with tears in her eyes, staring down at the little piece of paper in front of her, unable to use it. Her teacher, who was kind, gave her a stub of chalk and allowed Miel to write on the blackboard, but in a week or two, as soon as Miel went over the edge, the kindness stopped and Miel was punished with a ruler and then a yardstick, and then the dreaded paddling began. But the day she began to write on the ground nothing could stop her, they had to let a thing like that go. Soon the hallway floors of her school were covered with Miel's little exercises, which stayed there just long enough for her teachers to read them, correct them, grade them and call for the janitor to come mop them up. By the time she earned her certificate, the letters had stopped growing and were the same size as the ones I saw as a child, when I would lie down inside of her Os like a baby. Sadly, her letters were too long to keep, sometimes twenty-five feet or longer, and after an hour or two, before the men came home and the street was needed for their passing, my mother and her friends would tear Aunt Miel's letters along the lines of the original sheets she had pasted together, and every woman would take an armload home to burn in her stove. But the Thursdays they came were wonderful days, days I shall never forget, with my mother up on our roof, and all of the women in the neighborhood alerted by her standing there that a letter had come, and then the communal reading would begin, and it was a sight, what with the skirts and dresses and aprons billowing out on the roofs and fire escapes and balconies, and all of the heads hanging out of the windows, and Aunt Miel's life utterly exposed to the world, while the children below couldn't care a jot, and were happy and safe and warm, just finding a letter they could crawl into and call their own.

A ROMANTIC POET AND HIS DESTINY

Born into a family, H enjoyed an abundance of comforts and was provided a sound education, thanks to his uncle. Upon entering the world of commerce, H did not like banking, he did not like retailing, and he did not like practicing the law. What H liked were daughters. They liked H too, but not as much as they liked the phrase *auf wiedersehen*. Failure and rejection fertilized H. He wandered here and there, across hills and through valleys, composing songs. As time passed, little H became big. People tried to find him. He gravitated toward fountains and promoted their fallen charms. This shift in his writing style did not really change the world. Secret French money kept him alive—albeit he was surrounded by German spies. Living a tricky life was tiresome, so every seven months for seven years he cleared the skies with an illiterate girl. She convinced him to turn forty-four, but sadly he was confined to bed thereafter, by what the Germans call the French malady and the French call the German disease. He married the dear girl, often eating crackers in bed and writing on napkins. After he died, his whole estate went to his widow on the condition she would marry again so there would be at least one man to regret his passing.

IF ALL THE WORLD WERE PAPER

If you bother to read this at all it is a clear indication your life is intolerable and you seek a distraction by engaging in the activity you are presently pretending to engage in. I say *pretending* because you would never have reached the conclusion your life is intolerable had you not also reached the conclusion it is unreal. But long before one of the living comes to such a conclusion—that life is unreal—he first passes through the conclusion that reading is unreal, unreal because it is literally an imaginative act, so much so that no one *actually* reads, and has not *actually* read since they first learned how, compounded, of course, by the present-day fact no one "actually" reads anymore anyway. But little do any of your problems bother me on such a fine day! And it *is* a fine day, a fine day in plain view to anyone who happens to look up from their reading. All day I look at the grass. A woman in a big hat walks by. I sneeze. Occasionally I feel I am being born. At such moments of birth I am seized by a feeling of frightening abundance. There are too many trees in the world. There are too many trees and too many people, far too many people; there is too much shampoo and too much toothpaste, too much pollution, dirt, rocks and grass—far too much grass. The birds—too many of them fly. Don't bother counting, you'll never come to an end. Ditto pencils and pens. Don't mention books! Have you come to the part where I am only pretending to write? Surely you can tell I am only pretending to write. This is what pretending to write looks like, it looks like this. Not a landscape and yet passing before your eyes, unrolling as featureless as a plain and often you are the antelope, scared to have been born under such dismal skies. And you, aren't you only pretending to read? Yes, I can feel it, I can feel your eyes on my back, and I grant you, antelope, I am afraid, and the only way I can control my fear—of you pretending to read—is to go on pretending to write, and so long as I go on, you too shall go on. Isn't existence grand, the grandest bond between two you can imagine? Doesn't it outstrip your finest memory? Memories are worthless, have you ever stopped to consider that? Do you remember being by the seashore and watching the great broom of the sea come sweeping down on the shore, pushing all the glinty particles of sand out of its way? The sound of the sea's broom was so tremendous it sloshed the fluid in your ears. What did you come to the beach for anyway? Summer reading? What a pretense! Reading can't slosh the fluid in your ears the way a wave can. And the equatorial grass of the dunes looks and grows as a woman's hair when it is long and dry and white as parsnips. Parsnips, cut into disks and sautéed with an onion and a little garlic in a green pool of olive oil, could fool anyone into thinking they were something finer, nobler, more expensive and rare, not unlike the experience of dining on a well-prepared rabbit. The rabbit, another exquisite subject one could write a book about! One wonders, for example, whether there are more rabbits in the world than books, or more books than rabbits. Either way, what has happened to the world since its inception is condensed in the specimen of a single hare. It is real and it has reproduced itself, eaten parsnips and grasses, and been condemned to die at a railroad crossing. Soon the trains, too, shall pass out of all being, while books, I'm afraid, will go on pretending they are still among us. My friend—for nothing hinders me from calling you my friend, especially the fact we have never met, and are only now pretending to—if all the world were made of paper, and perhaps it is, it could one day conceivably burn for years, like the rainforests of Brazil were once so fond of doing, and eventually we'd be reduced to a few square heaps of ash, as if the sun had strayed too close, or one among us drifted too far, the sensitivity of his organs of perception so extreme he regarded all of civilization, and most of literature, an illusion.

A MINOR PERSONAL MATTER

For a long time I was a poet. That is, I used to be a poet, for quite a long time in fact, and made my life making poems and teaching persons younger than myself just what this entailed, although I myself had no idea what it entailed, beyond a certain amount of courage and a certain amount of fear, but these amounts were variable and it was not always possible to say in which order they appeared and at any rate it was hard to convey. It was harder and harder to convey, but conveying it became easier and easier and that, too, lent an air of confusion to my days. For instance, many days I did not care about saying any of this, I only cared to say certain things that might cause someone to like me, but of course I never said that. I said only that I cared to say certain things that might cause someone to like the language. This seemed foolish because whether or not someone liked the language they had no choice but to use it. Whether or not the language was beautiful or gruff or strange they had no choice but to use it. So I said I only cared to say certain things that might cause someone to like the world, and being alive in it. This seemed foolish because whether or not someone liked the world they had no choice but to live in it. Whether the world was beautiful or gruff or strange they had no choice but to live. Yes, I said, you may kill yourself, but that would not be living, you would not be living then. A great many poets killed themselves. This was a problem too insurmountable to even understand, although at times I felt I understood it very closely and this also was part of the problem. The only thing that seemed certain to me was that people who had no choice but to use the language while they were alive had a choice in whether or not they liked me. This was a real choice, one I might be able to persuade them in. And so it seemed to me this reason, the one which sounded most foolish of all (and therefore I never spoke it) was actually the most reasonable of all. Still, occasionally I met people who did not seem to like me no matter what I said or did. And it was not easy to turn away from them because they were the challenge. They were the challenge because they challenged me to like myself even if they did not. That was the challenge—to like myself in spite of all that happened or did not happen to me. It was to face this challenge that I ceased to write poems. Could I like myself if I no longer engaged in an activity I openly declared was the reason I was put on the planet in the first place? Would I find another reason to be on the planet, or could I remain on the planet, with nothing to do and no one to like me, liking myself? I decided to try. I was on the planet with nothing to do and no one to like me. And as soon as I found myself there, I realized I had created the circumstances in which I had begun to write poems in the first place, to the extent I now wander the earth, a ghost, with no intent to write, but carrying a spark in my fingertips, which keeps me in a state of constant fibrillation, neither dead nor alive, a will-o'-the-wisp of stress, art, and the hours.

ON TWILIGHT

I read the poem of a student and in the poem God wandered through a room picking up random objects—a pear, a vase, a shoe—and in bewilderment said, "I made this?" Apparently God had forgotten making anything at all. I awarded this poem a prize, because I was a judge of such matters. I was not really awarding the student, I was awarding God; I knew someday the student would pick up his old poem and say in bewilderment, "I made this?", and at that moment his whole world would be lost in the twilight, and when you are finally lost in the twilight, you cannot judge anything.

UNIVERSITY OF THE LIMITLESS MOUSE

The University of the Limitless Mouse was more or less like any other university, except for exams: students sat for suet every four months, eating a block of it, spitting the seeds into little cups passed out for that purpose, and were given a bar of motel soap for washing their hands afterwards. Those unfortunates who swallowed the seeds grew into huge and solitary trees whose sole purpose was to shade the campus from anything that might come to it from above. The provost liked particularly the roots of these trees and saw to it they were strong. The day did come however when *the old pumpkin fricasseed in snow* (as he liked to call himself in a show of learning) died, and not long afterward the academy closed out of respect for the melancholy. The tree roots, which had risen above ground like enormous braids of bread dough, shrank back to withered veins. The limitless supply of mice, no longer instructed or even able to lose themselves in the great maze of roots, stretched to the horizon, and it was here, among them, I now wandered, one to whom it had always been curious that the failed, the seed-swallowers, should have been so favored, though none of the other mice shared my curiosity, and indeed, on the point of starving, they now began to devour the entire system of roots down to six million pounds of what, in the final stages of that learned feast, looked like ash. And so it was that I alone passed down the road of questioning, which was deserted and giving out black smoke from those broken individuals, about whom so little is known and so much has been written.

SOME NONDESCRIPT AUTUMN WEEKEND

Remove everything beautiful from your home, remove everything you like, love, cherish or are fond of. Remember to include pets and people. Remove everything which reminds you of these things in any way. Remove everything which brings you happiness or a feeling of peace. Remove everything which reminds you of your life.

Leave everything which you feel is ugly, disgusting, broken or painful. Leave everything that makes you uncomfortable when you look at it or use it. If necessary, add to these things by bringing more of them from the outside in. Make sure your home is as full as it once was and be certain everything is crummy and repulsive. Live in this space, among these things you cannot bear, for sixty days.

Empty the space completely. Leave nothing in it. Clean it thoroughly and wash the windows. Sleep on the floor, or on a clean thin mattress the exact dimensions of your own body. Live in this space for sixty days, during which your primary activity, when you are home, is to stare at the ceiling.

Bring the beautiful things back in, bring your beloved belongings, your most cherished possessions, back into the space and place them in their original positions. Make sure everything is as it was before. Live as you once did; if this is not possible, live twice.

A HALF-SKETCHED HEAD

THIS IS WHY

It was of no use, trying to discern whether the anchorite was happy or unhappy; in the first days of her visit Mary assumed this was why she had come, but the longer she stayed the more she felt at home, the more she felt at home, the more she felt free to be miserable, and finally Mary saw that the question was useless.

REGRETS

The anchorite was in the habit of keeping lists. Among them Mary noticed a continuing list of regrets, under that heading, and though many of them were crossed off or blackened out, new ones were added as well. Mary asked him if a kind of balance were kept, to which he replied: "If only! As a matter of fact, your question is an item I have been tempted to add to the list."

CHILDHOOD MEMORIES

There was a long silence during which he seemed to be struggling. Suddenly he looked up at her. "I wish to tell you as quickly as possible that when I was a boy it was my sole responsibility to feed the baby goats from a bottle containing their mother's milk. On one such occasion I managed to spill the goat's milk down my shirtfront—over which I should have been wearing a smock in the first place. And though I can't tell you why, I was wearing my best shirt: perhaps for the like of that alone I deserved to be punished. I went immediately to the washroom and began to rinse out the milk spots, using a large bar of my mother's soap, which was always in plentiful supply since she made it herself. And as I stood there it struck me—my mother's soap was goat's milk soap, with goat's milk I was trying desperately to erase goat's milk. That something could be its own remedy—though I did not then think in those terms—struck me as a rather serious joke. It was my first occasion of panic."

MOMENTS OF DELIGHT

Once Mary found his shopping list—it was written on a pink slip from one of those rainbow pads: *trout, staplegun, cherries, hammer, ribbon, wire.* "Ah, that summer," he said, "that summer. I sought perfection in all things. When a few groceries were needed I would spend hours devising—then revising—the list. Then in the store I carried it crunched in my hand, filled with an excruciating fear: the fear that others would discover, perhaps in the checkout line, that my list was less perfect than theirs."

AGAIN

On the second occasion of Mary's finding a shopping list—this one pinned under the weight of an extra-large egg snug in its styrofoam socket—the anchorite chanced to see her with it. Peering over her shoulder he read *rhubarb, roses, crab legs, gray socks,* then turned to her and said "Isn't that the fate, Madam, of one destined to think in scraps?" What follows are a few of those scraps, thrown to Mary while she did what few chores needed to be done while tending to the anchorite, who was ailing at that time.

RELIGION

Whatever habit one is most faithful to—whatever one does most, loves best, is their religion. A simple matter of precedence.

PENANCE

Penance is the heart of the matter. Why do any of us live the way we do? It is why I live here, in the middle of nowhere. Precisely, it is the penance for never having sinned.

PRAYER

Can we conceive of a religion without prayer? And what, exactly, is prayer? If I am in prayer I seem to be concentrated. But I seem to be concentrating now and I am certainly not in prayer. What then is peculiar to one's concentration in prayer? It seems, simply, that one must concentrate on something that doesn't exist, as in prayers to our Lord, or prayers for the future—prayers for a turn of events, against all odds. What counts is that it does not exist. In which case, algebra seems a very good way to get to heaven.

AN ASIDE

It would be best if one could not hear oneself pray, since one always tends to eavesdrop on their own conversations with God, as though neither of the parties were oneself.

HANDS

It is true I once spent some time in a novitiate. One evening after supper there was a lively conversation concerning whether the ideal hands for prayer should be gloved or ungloved. I suggested that they be disembodied.

"Do you yourself pray—now?" Mary asked.

"My hands pray."

"And what do they pray for?"

"My hands pray to be kept on!"

FAITH OF THE LEGGED

What is the fascination, throughout history, with birds? Is it that they cannot fall? It is just this that the legged envy. If no bird was ever known to sing a song, what difference would be had, since the legged can sing as well? But only the legged can fall. Perhaps the legged sing because they can fall, and the birds sing because they cannot fall, and the fascination with birds, throughout history, is a difference in causation of song. In which case I see that I was not originally wrong. You see, Mary, despite the fact I am legged and can fall, I am never wrong.

HIS TATTOO

Mary noticed a small door, slightly ajar, etched on the left side of his chest.

HIS MOTTO

"I disappear."

Mary learned the anchorite was a great believer in mottoes. He dreamt of a world in which mottoes were given in place of names. In such a world, the mere presentation or introduction of one person to another would result in effortless conversation:

"Capable of Dissembling"
"I build"
"Free from all pastimes"
"With honor and valor"
"I disappear"

MARY'S MOTTO

At the the end of the first year of their acquaintance the anchorite gave Mary a motto. It has been a difficult decision, he said, for he wished to bond them through similar mottoes yet bestow Mary with her own characteristics.

He finally decided upon "I disappoint."

ON SEX

Just as one lover can be better than another it seems possible that one celibate might be... more accomplished... than the next. In this vein, I consider myself the greatest of all celibates.

NEWS

"Look here," the anchorite said one day, "I have been reading about a new abyss."
"What's that?" asked Mary.
"The Eucharist is acidic and will upset an ulcer."

SUNDAY PAPER

One Sunday in June he was reading the book review and noticed an author's query, "I would be grateful for information on the life and work of the Spanish painter Maruja Mallo (1902–95)." He thought he would submit an author's query himself, asking gratefully for any information others might have pertaining to his own life and work, giving his own name and the date of his birth. In this way he thought he could learn a good deal more about himself than he already knew, for recent events had led him to realize he was not so well-informed as he had imagined. Proof of this, he told Mary, was the fact he could not even say what these recent events were.

SHAKESPEARE

In the same newspaper he saw an ad for *The Complete Penguin Shakespeare* and he thought it very odd that penguins would bother to read Shakespeare at all.

INCOGNITO

Some of us are happy living a double life, and some of us are tortured by it—though for those there is always the hope that our doubleness will consist in being both of these persons.

CONVERSION

The anchorite ate a single fried egg each morning, just as the sun came up. One morning, while seasoning his egg, he told Mary how he had come to have faith: he simply realized that he had never—not once—refilled his salt and pepper shakers, which he had used profusely for twenty years.

RESPONSIBILITY

God is a toddler. He is learning to walk, tumbling into everything, touching the luminous red surface, surface of your innermost thoughts like coils on a hotplate. He has got to learn. It is up to you to teach him.

HOMUNCULUS

I believe it was Chekhov who said there should be a little man with a hammer in the heads of happy persons, to remind them of the poor and famished. A noble thought... but the little man is also a member of the Guilt Berets, and the spiritually fortified should be able to be happy in the midst of great squalor, disappointment, and the most ghastly circumstances. Thus the homunculus must be shot.

IMPERSONAL PROBLEMS

Sometimes I think I am of a species that is bored to extinction, or that I am the last of such a species whose predominant trait was boredom. Nothing modern mind you—not in the least. Just an oversized head that looks up as soon as it gets dark and is heard to remark "Heigh-ho little moon, heigh-ho!" Wherein completes the activity of an evening.

ON WOMEN

I met a twenty-first-century French feminist literary critic who said "How can women describe their feelings in a language that was primarily devised by men to describe theirs?" I told her the truth—that that was a direct quote from Thomas Hardy.

LARGE, SAD NUMBERS

Which number is greater—the number of poems collected and preserved by man, or the number of poems thrown away by the women who wrote them? And if the lesser poems outnumber the greater poems, consider this: is it sadder to read such poems or to write them?

TRICK OR TREAT

My head is like a pumpkin with eyes; both hollow and lit. Hollow except for a few seeds, left over from my birth, and long bits of stringy, mashed flesh—yet someone, who is most definitely not myself, has placed a candle there. It positively glows.

HOW FINELY WE ARGUE UPON MISTAKEN FACTS!

ON PRIVACY

Imagine the man who, after having made the world, consented to become a carpenter! I'm led to believe there was a want of privacy. In other words, I'm led to believe there is absolutely no substitute for a human lifetime.

THE MAGNIFYING GLASS

Mary noticed the anchorite did not wear spectacles, nor was there any evidence of such a need. But one large magnifying glass he did keep, and used to distinguish anything he himself had put to ink. "Can't you read your own writing?" she asked, pointing to the magnifying glass. "Oh, that," he said, "it's because my thoughts are so small."

BOOKS

I've read a few, but as for scholars, professors, intellectuals, academics, authors and poets, historians and philosophers—now there's a lot I can't get close to. Their lives would not exist without their books. How they must suffer from an overdose of masterpieces! My idea is... memorize as much as you can and forget the rest. Heigh-ho little moon!

ON POETRY

Poets are so coarsely bred they believe in force-feeding, arranged marriages, predestined outbursts. Any two tricks between words will do. It's true, I, too, delight in being vulgar. Yet once I was a boy of five years and one place, I didn't even know the word Poetry existed; I had never read a poem: what did I do then? I went fishing! I lived in a trout's world, that strange underwater adagio. A slow circle. And now I think of it... so poetically! Haven't I then been two completely different persons? And lived in at least two worlds? China trees, cinnamon trees, cypress and spindle-wood, the ash tree and the holly bush: some dog has shat on them all. The true trouble with poetry is simple: it depends on distraction to survive. And if God is a poet then I *am* afraid—for it is frightening to think that He is a no one, and speaks not from Himself, but from the character He has found in me.

ART HISTORY

In Bruges, in the eighteenth century, they sold the shutters of a triptych by Gerard David at the request of the sacristan, who objected to the trouble of opening and closing them, complaining that they broke the altar candles each time he did so. Wise man.

FAVORITE PRAYER

Lord, let nothing get behind me.

DARK MOOD

In a dark mood, I lie down on the ground and the sun that has reached the earth and sunk into it rises up through the ground and enters my back. Nothing comes from above.

TIME TRAVEL

To be transposed to ancient Egypt! It would be like opening the door to my own home, for theirs was a great culture, entirely dedicated to pretending to be dead.

DREAM

A very old librarian with the kind of blue eyes that absorb nothing but reflect everything. The kind you cannot look at, the blueblind eyes of a psychic or beauty queen. She had skin like a fine handkerchief that has been folded many times, smelled faintly of talcum, and wore a rhinestone flower on her lapel. She was in fact the world's expert on violets. She was very sweet to me and gave me a tour of the library which lasted from sunrise to sunset—that's how large the library was. She listened politely while I explained to her that I was only an anchorite with a very small IQ and could not possibly read all the books in her library or even understand them and that the tour, though finely given, had somewhat depressed me. I felt she had wasted her time, and I was sorry. She was even more polite, and infinitely sweeter, when she explained my mistake. These are the books, she said, that have yet to be written, how could anyone read them?

SEQUEL TO A DREAM

The very next night the librarian came back to me, for she had forgotten to tell me something of the utmost importance. She said violets are more common in English literature than the rose, a little known fact that was nonetheless true, and if I thought about this bit of information for long enough it was the equivalent of reading all the books in any earthly library and all those in her own. She told me this with great tact and compassion, as if offering me a little aspirin in the palm of her hand.

INTELLECTUAL FATE

Once I was face to face with a great snowy owl. As it happened I said to myself this will never happen again. Such a sad reaction! The bird flew off before I could have any other. This is an example of my intellectual fate. I have no memory of the bird whatsoever, and it never happened again.

ON BEARS

The anchorite wanted most to know what the bear felt like upon first awakening from his hibernation. When Mary asked him to elaborate he replied, "That is precisely the question I have in mind: is it an elaborate moment for the bear, or is it essentially spare? Anchored and massive, or does he feel—wouldn't it be delightful—like a fly in a cathedral?"

ON CANCER

We are the brain tumor of the earth. Because of us she wanders the universe with a shaved head, full of spleen, without a cure. One day she will lose the words for *white hawthorn, black locust, Dutch elm*. Then *periwinkle* will be gone. She will, undoubtedly, still spin. The sound of a Coke bottle being opened on the next planet will bring some momentary sense into her days: she will remember the word for *fizz*. And when she dies, who will be seen squinting at her grave?

ON SYMBOLS

"I don't know of any," he said.

AGE

How odd the years are. If we were thermometers no one would want to be 30; everyone would want to be 78.

PAST LIVES

I am reasonably assured that I was Philip the Assured, who in 1467 was the richest prince in Europe and shut himself up in a little workshop to spend his remaining days fitting together pieces of broken glass. They buried him in St. Donatian's and so great was the throng at his funeral, and the heat engendered by thousands of candles, that they shattered the gorgeous stained glass windows to let in air.

GIFT

Mary asked about the fig tree in his garden. "It was a gift," he said, "from, shall we say, an anchoress I once knew. I dare say she knew exactly what she was presenting me with: the fig tree, as you know, has had an illustrious past: Buddha attained enlightenment under its kin, while Jesus made one barren. Have I then been blessed or cursed?"

BONSAI

Though sometimes it is simple, it is never easy—to be alone and thinking of nothing. In the bonsai brain, there is no branch so old, and none so small, that from time to time it doesn't do something peculiar!

THE PICKING

I picked a bouquet of twenty lady's slippers, the genitalia of spring, which are an endangered species in these parts. They sat on my desk in a paper cup and gave me great joy. The following year our spring woods, devoid of any such mauve, gave me an even greater thrill.

FAVORITE NOVEL

The book whose every page is turned by Satan's breath! The most ill-mannered, violent, demented book ever written—and by a lady! Can you guess? No, Mary, you're much too dull to know I mean *Wuthering Heights*. And need I remind you of the opening lines of Chapter Ten: "A charming introduction to a hermit's life! Four weeks' torture, tossing, and sickness!"

DECONSTRUCTION

I think the sirens in *The Odyssey* sang *The Odyssey*, for there is nothing more seductive, more terrible, than the story of our own life, the one we do not want to hear and will do anything to listen to.

ONE BOOK

How many books have I read? Only one—just as anyone who is literate has read only one book, or, to be precise, is in the process of reading the one book they will complete in their lifetime. That book is the particular sum of every book they have ever read, written in the particular order in which those books were read. The book is never the same, for no two persons have ever read exactly the same books in exactly the same order. There is a great difference between *The Password to Larkspur Lane* followed by *Anna Karenina* and *Anna Karenina* followed by *The Password to Larkspur Lane*. And if *What One Can Do With a Chafing Dish* happens to fall between... as opposed to *Don Quixote*... well, I don't mean to insult the genetic researchers, but I have a hunch that if no two people are alike, this is why.

ILLITERATES

There are no illiterates! What you call an illiterate is simply someone who has had the time to read the greatest books of all—a bush, a bird, a toe, a star—so that the same principle of a single book applies. The difference you seek is between those who don't understand what they read, and those who do. Now I ask you, to which of these persons does the greatest pleasure belong? That is the interesting question.

EXCEPTION

Why is it we speak of unreliable narrators, but not of unreliable readers? A reader freely judges the author, but the author is not allowed to judge the reader. Except, of course, in the Bible.

WORST YEARS

Mary asked which were the worst years of his life. "Well, there have been two *bad* years—1951 and 1976. Particularly dry springs—no morels, my dear."

LATE-BREAKING NEWS

My latest occasion of panic was not so far removed from the goat's milk episode of my youth; ten days ago I realized I was sobbing in a Saab.

IT MAY BE

It may be, in an occasional pew, wisdom independent of thought arises: you ought to think deeply about this. There are not, as I once thought, a variety of ways in which we think. I began to worry that I was thinking less and fantasizing more. Until I realized that all thinking is fantasy—the reductionist, structuralist, logician, the computer and the dreamer... they are all fantasizing!

END RESULT

You should know there have been several opinions as to what makes the homo sapiens distinct. But I think these can be safely reduced to three: his ability to think symbolically, his ability to be bored, and the capacity, in all ages and in all places, for intoxication: corn, palm, sugarcane, vine, curl of the tobacco leaf, poppy unfurled! The holy trinity of what makes man man, woman woman: isn't it sad and ridiculous that according to such criteria the classic human being would be the bored drunk writing poetry? And if I may carry the results further we may distill the distinctions to poetry alone, symbolic thinking which first intoxicates and then bores.

REGRETS

That I am not an electron—lightest of all particles—lightest and lightest of mass—and still to be!

LIVES OF SAINTS AND SAILORS

If people want to touch my body after I am dead, I ask that they refrain from such shameful activity. However, they may kiss the back of my neck as many times as they want, after I am dead, in token of the fact they did not do this to me while I was living.

ON BURIAL

There are only two tombs: the tomb of Jesus and the tomb of Tut. Roll away one stone and you will be given everything: food, clothing, shelter, gems, cloth, seeds and oil, a replica of the world in pure gold. Roll away the other stone and there's nothing.

MY PRIVATE PROPERTY

For Michael

"The cumbersome bones, the curious distance from foot and fingertip to brain, too; and those quarts and quarts of blood. I shuddered. It was little short of a miracle that they escaped continual injury; and what an extended body in which to die."

— Walter de la Mare, *Memoirs of a Midget*

LITTLE GOLF PENCIL

At headquarters they asked me for something dry and understated. Mary, they said, it's called a *statement*. They took me out back to a courtyard where they always ate lunch and showed me a little tree that was, sadly, dying. Something with four legs had eaten it rather badly. Don't over-emote, they said. I promised I wouldn't but I was thinking to myself that the something-with-four-legs had certainly over-emoted and that the tree, in response, was over-emoting now, being in the strange little position of dying. All the cops were sitting around eating sandwich halves and offered me one. This one's delicious, said a lieutenant, my wife made it. Seeing as it was peanut butter and jelly I thought he was over-emoting, but I didn't say anything. I just sat looking at the tree and eating my sandwich half. When I was ready I asked for a pencil and they gave me one of those little golf pencils. I didn't say anything about that, either. I just wrote my statement and handed it over—it was a description of the tree which they intended to give to their captain as a Christmas present—I mean my description, not the tree—because the captain, well, he loved that tree and he loved my writing and every one of the cops hoped to be promoted in the captain's heart and, who knows, maybe get a raise. Still, after all that sitting around in the courtyard eating sandwich halves, I had a nice feeling of sharing, so when they asked me whether I had anything else to say I told them that in the beginning you understand the world but not yourself, and when you finally understand yourself you no longer understand the world. They seemed satisfied with that. Cops, they're all so young.

KEYS

Poor little keys! Success is not always to be expected, for passive resistance having become the creed of keys, it takes the form of what their tormentors call obstinacy, and when it has become hereditary, I am afraid all the world won't get it out of them. All that can be done is to rescue a solitary individual now and then, and try what care and kindness may make of him. Not long ago, shocked at the cruelty with which they were treated, a benevolent gentleman, who had his theories about keys, determined that he would bring up a young key as one raises a young child. A little one was brought, and kept in a hole, but when the time came the key would not come out of his hole, and nothing would ever make him. The key's feelings were those of a snail being pulled from his shell. What became of that key was never known, but it seems certain one hole led to another, and it is my deepest hope that the benevolent gentleman let him live by trying him in ever other holes, and that eventually there passed between them an authentic feeling, even if it was one of defeat.

PLEASE READ

"Once upon a time there was a bird, my God."
— Clarice Lispector

I am the yellow finch that came to her feeder an hour before she died. I was the last living thing she saw, so my responsibility was great. Yet all I did was eat. Through eight long months of winter the black oiled sunflower seeds had gone untouched—not a single one of my kind or any other kind had approached them. It was too much work. Even if we'd had the strength—which we did not, half-starved as we were—we were not in the mood to crack anything. On the morning of the twenty-second of April she took them away and refilled the feeding tube with sunflower hearts—sheeny niblets whose hard outer husk had been stripped away by some faraway, intricate machine. She went back inside and waited. From my branch I could see her do the things she liked to do—she picked up a towel from off the floor, she filled out a card stopping the mail, she boiled water, she stared into space. She saw me coming. Her face flickered with, if not exactly joy, the ordinary wellspring of life. It's true there was a sheet of glass between us. But I could see the seeds of her eyes and the upturned corners of her mouth. I ate a heart. I turned my head. She looked at me as if I were the last living thing on earth. And as I was, I kept on eating.

LUCKY

While I was sleeping God broke into my heart and nailed up pictures of Himself in different clothes. He asked me which one I liked the best, but it was apparent I was to like them all. I didn't like any of them, but there was one, a white robe with a floating blue halo above the neckline where His face should be, and I thought to that picture I could at least express my Fear. So I said I liked it. Immediately He said that I had no taste. I thought I would wake then and there, with a bad taste in my mouth, and choose for the day brightly colored clothes of the kind I would never wear, but that didn't happen. I slept dreamless as a baby, and when I awoke I was naked as a baby, and alone, and afraid.

OBSERVATIONS ON THE GROUND

The planet seen from extremely close up is called the *ground*. The ground can be made loose by the human hand, or by using a small tool held in the human hand, such as a *spade*, or an even larger tool, such as a *shovel*, or a variety of machines commonly called *heavy equipment*. We bury our dead in the ground. Roughly half the dead are buried in boxes and half the dead are buried without boxes. A burying box is an emblem of respect for the dead. We are the only species to so envelop our dead. An earlier, more minimal, way to envelop the dead was to wrap them in cloth.

Besides burying the dead in the ground, we bury our garbage, also called *trash*. Man-made mountains of garbage are pushed together using heavy equipment and then pushed down into the ground. The site of this burial is called a *landfill*. The site of the dead buried in boxes is called a *cemetery*. In both cases the ground is being filled. A dead body in a box can be lowered into the ground using heavy equipment, but we do not consider it trash. When the dead are not in boxes and there is a man-made mountain of them we use heavy equipment to bury them together, like trash. It is estimated that everywhere we walk we are walking on a piece of trash and the hard, insoluble remains of the dead. Whatever the case, the dead and the garbage are together in the ground where we cannot see them, for we do not relish the sight or smell of them. If we did not go about our burying, we would be in danger of being overcome.

Also buried in the ground are *seeds*, which we want to see when they emerge from the ground in their later form—that is, as *plants*. Plants rising from the ground are essential to life. To bury a seed is to *plant* it. When a seed is planted and not seen again, those who buried it are made sad. The anticipated plant of the wished-upon seed has not materialized. It is dead, and remains buried. Heavy equipment is used to plant large expanses of ground with seed. When a whole field of shivering grain rises from the earth, there is a growing sense of happiness among those who buried the seeds. Happiness is also present when a tree emerges, or a tree that will bear fruit, or leafy green, edible plants that were formerly planted. When *flowers* arise from the ground, colorful and shapely in an astonishing variety of ways, the living are made *especially* happy. Not only are flowers admired for their outward beauty of form, their scents are capable of overcoming us and therefore prized. Nothing, it seems, makes the living as happy as a flower. Flowers are among the most anticipated things on earth. For this reason, we separate the flower from the ground and present it to another to hold or to look at. After a while, the flower that has been separated from the ground *dies*, and we throw it in the trash. Flowers are often planted where the dead are buried in boxes, but these flowers are *never* cut. That would be *horrible*. Whoever did such a thing would be considered a *thief*. *Those* flowers belong to the dead.

Blue sadness is sweetness cut into strips with scissors and then into little pieces by a knife, it is the sadness of reverie and nostalgia: it may be, for example, the memory of a happiness that is now only a memory, it has receded into a niche that cannot be dusted for it is beyond your reach; distinct and dusty, blue sadness lies in your inability to dust it, it is as unreachable as the sky, it is a fact reflecting the sadness of all facts. Blue sadness is that which you wish to forget, but cannot, as when on a bus one suddenly pictures with absolute clarity a ball of dust in a closet, such an odd, unshareable thought that one blushes, a deep rose spreading over the blue fact of sadness, creating a situation that can only be compared to a temple, which exists, but to visit it one would have to travel two thousand miles on snowshoes and by dogsled, five hundred by horseback and another five hundred by boat, with a thousand by rail.

THE WOMAN WHO COULDN'T DESCRIBE A THING IF SHE COULD

We have a house. There is a roof and there are windows. I think they are square. You can see through them, that's for sure. There is a door to go into and out of the house. It works both ways. And oh, a floor.

We left the house in a car. The car had wheels, there were four of them. And there was a door for going into and out of the car. Actually there were four doors, there were four of us, too, so we each had our own door. Inside there was only room to sit down, and a strap that went across your body in case there was an accident.

An accident is when something happens that is not supposed to happen and you don't want it to but it does anyway. We did not have an accident that day. We went to a restaurant instead.

The car stayed outside the restaurant and we stayed inside the restaurant. A restaurant is a place that will cook for you. You give them money for the cooking. Or for the eating, I am unsure which.

You probably already know this, but eating is when the food goes inside your body. Later it comes out a different door in another way. (When I said the car had four doors I forgot number five, the little door where the gas goes in.)

So we four were in the restaurant. Some of the food was good and some of the food was bad, but it costs the same.

As you eat you have a conversation. A conversation is talking between people. One person said "I am tired of the heat," and another said "Me too." I said "I kind of like it." The last of us said "Could we talk about something other than the weather?" I thought that was an interesting thing to say.

A thought is silent talking to yourself in your head. But you can still hear it. This is the number-one difference.

After the eating and the conversation, one of us gave money for these things. You just hand it over and for a moment you can see it, it is moving from one hand to another hand and you can see it, it is paper. But it is not usually shown, most of the time you keep your money out of sight. It is hardly ever in the air. It is not like a necklace or something. But at such and such a time you take it out and give some of it away. You never give your necklace away. All the same a necklace is a sign of money. It just is. You show the sign that you have things hidden. It goes back and forth, like a conversation.

Two of us were wearing necklaces and two of us were not. That is a fact I added together later, so you would know.

We left the restaurant by the door. There was the car. In the car we did not have a conversation. We left the car when it was looking at the house.

Inside the house there was an accident. Accidents happen so fast you never really see them, so no one can really talk about them. After the accident there was another conversation. It was longer than the conversation we had in the restaurant, even though there were four of us in the restaurant and now there were only three.

Then it was time for bed. A bed is where you sleep. If you have a necklace you take it off. Both you and the necklace change from an upright position to a downright position. But not together.

You close your eyes, which have been open all day. You close your mouth, which has been open all day. You think about the day. You have the whole day all to yourself. Then you begin to see things inside your head which you did not put there. It is very dark outside your head and you cannot see much there, but you can see the "put" things inside your head. When that happens, you know you are asleep. You might not know it, but you are.

You are asleep. The day is done. You can't describe it anymore. That's life. It's over.

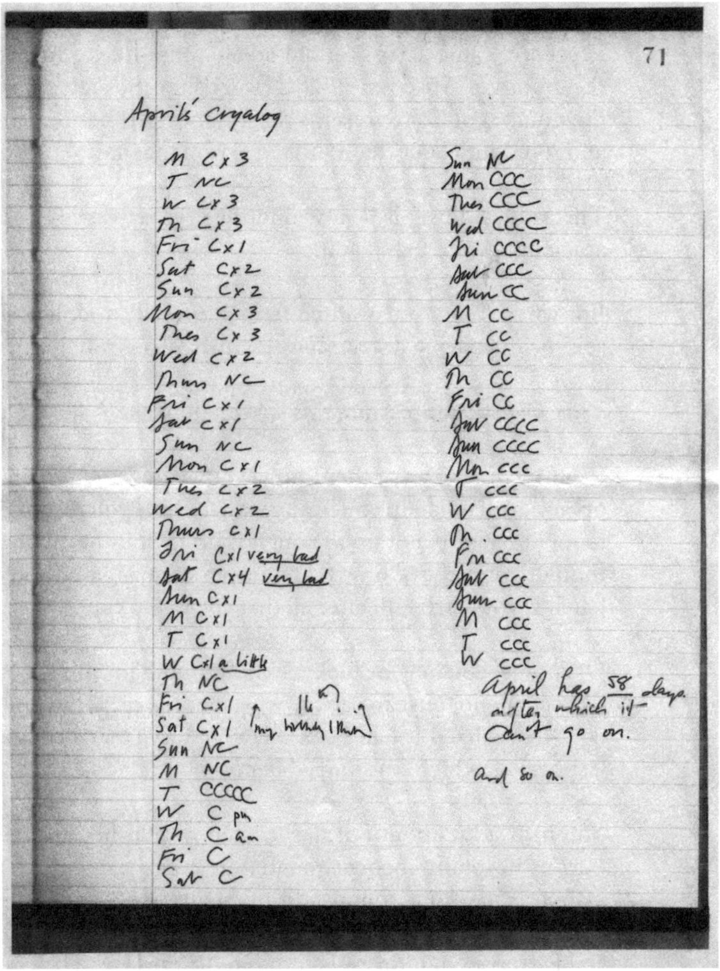

71

April's cryalog

M Cx3
T NC
W Cx3
Th Cx3
Fri Cx1
Sat Cx2
Sun Cx2
Mon Cx3
Tues Cx3
Wed Cx2
Thurs NC
Fri Cx1
Sat Cx1
Sun NC
Mon Cx1
Tues Cx2
Wed Cx2
Thurs Cx1
Fri Cx1 very bad
Sat Cx4 very bad
Sun Cx1
M Cx1
T Cx1
W Cx1 a little
Th NC
Fri Cx1 16th? my birthday I think
Sat Cx1
Sun NC
M NC
T CCCCC
W C pm
Th C am
Fri C
Sat C

Sun NC
Mon CCC
Tues CCC
Wed CCCC
Fri CCCC
Sat CCC
Sun CC
M CC
T CC
W CC
Th CC
Fri CC
Sat CCCC
Sun CCCC
Mon CCC
T CCC
W CCC
Th. CCC
Fri CCC
Sat CCC
Sun CCC
M CCC
T CCC
W CCC

April has 58 days.
after which it
can't go on.

And so on.

PAUSE

I recently came across an old cryalog that I kept during the month of April in 1998. "C" stands for the fact *I cried*, the number of Cs represents the number of times I cried, and "NC" indicates that I did not cry on that day.

The saddest thing is, I now find the cryalog very funny, and laugh when I look at it.

But when I kept it, I wanted to die. Literally, to kill myself–with an iron, a steaming-hot turned-on iron.

This was not depression, this was menopause.

Reading this, or any other thing ever written about menopause, will not help you in any way, for how you respond to menopause is not up to you, it is up to your body, and though you believe now that you can control your body (such is your strength after all that yoga) you cannot.

Of course, you may be lucky: I know a woman who experienced menopause in no way whatsoever except that one day she realized it had been a couple of years since her last period, which was indeed her *last*.

You hear a lot about hot flashes, but hot flashes are the *least* of it, totally inconsequential in every way: you get as hot as a steam iron at odd moments–so what? The media would have you believe that hot flashes are the single most significant symptom toward which you should direct your attention and *their* products, but when I think of menopause I don't think of hot flashes;

I am not here to talk about hot flashes.

Except to tell you that they do not cease even after you have completely gone through menopause; they become a part of your life the way your periods were, they are periodic and, after a while, you stop talking about them.

No, I am here to tell you that one woman, a woman who is the most undepressed, optimistic, upbeat person I know, awoke one morning and walked straight into her kitchen and grabbed a butcher's knife (she is a world-class cook) with the intent of driving it through her heart. That was menopause.

If you take the time to peruse the annals of any nineteenth-century asylum, as I have, you will discover that the "cause of admittance" for all women over forty is listed as *cessation of menses*. Sometimes I saw the words *change of life*, which sounds like a euphemism *but isn't*.

In other words, you go crazy. When you go crazy, you don't have the slightest inclination to read anything Foucault ever wrote about culture and madness.

It may be that you recall your thirteenth year on earth. Menopause is adolescence all over again, only you are an adult and have to go out into the world every day in ways you did not have to when you were in school, where you were surrounded by other adolescents, safe, or relatively so, in the asylum of junior high.

You are a thirteen-year-old with the experience and daily life of a forty-five-year-old.

You have on some days the desire to fuck a tree, or a dog, whichever is closest.

You have the desire to leave your husband or lover or partner, whatever.

No matter how stable or loving the arrangement, you want out.

You may decide to take up an insane and hopeless cause. You may decide to walk to Canada, or that it is high time you begin to collect old blue china, three thousand pieces of which will leave you bankrupt. Suddenly the solution to all problems lies in selling your grandmother's gold watch or drinking your body weight in cider vinegar. A kind of wild forest blood runs in your veins.

This, and other behaviors, will horrify you. You will seek medical help because you are intelligent, and none of the help will help.

You will feel as if your life is over and you will be absolutely right about that, it is over.

No matter how attractive or unattractive you are, you have been used to having others look you over when you stood at the bus stop or at the chemist's to buy tampons. They have looked you over to assess how attractive or unattractive you are, so no matter what the case, you were looked at. Those days are over; now others look straight through you, you are completely *invisible* to them, you have become a *ghost*.

You no longer exist.

Because you no longer exist, you will do anything for attention. You may shave your head or dye your hair or wear striped stockings or scream at complete strangers. You've seen them, haven't you, the middle-aged women screaming at the attendant in the convenience store?

You are a depressed adolescent who sweats through her clothing and says terrible things to everyone, especially the people she loves.

You begin to lie. You have the urge to shoplift, and if you drive an automobile you have the urge to ram your car into the car in front of you.

Nothing can prepare you for this.

The one thing no one will tell you is that these feelings and this behavior will last ten years. That is, a decade of your life. Ask your doctor if this is true and she will deny it.

Then comes a day when you see a "woman" who is buying tampons and you think of her as a *girl*. And she is; anyone who has periods is a girl. You know this is true and it is very funny to you.

You are a woman, the ten years have passed, you love your children, you love your lover, but there are no longer any persons on earth who can stop you from being yourself—you have put your parents in the earth, you have buried the past. Of course in the meantime you have destroyed your life and it has to be completely remade and there is a great deal of grief and regret and nostalgia and all of that, but even so you are free, free to sit on the bank and throw stones and feel thankful for the few years or one or two decades left to you in which you can be yourself, even if a great many other women ended their lives, even if the reason they ended their lives is reported as having been for reasons having nothing to do with menopause, which is thankfully behind you as you would never want to be a girl again for any reason at all, you have discovered that being *invisible* is the biggest secret on earth, the most wondrous gift anyone could ever have given you.

If you are young and you are reading this, perhaps you will understand the gleam in the eye of any woman who is sixty, seventy, eighty, or ninety: she cannot take you seriously (sorry) for you are but a girl to her, despite your babies and shoes and lovemaking and all of that. You are just a girl playing at life.

You are just a girl on the edge of a great forest. You should be frightened but instead you are eating a lovely meal, or you are cooking one, or you are running to the florist or you are opening a box of flowers that has just arrived at your door—and none of these things is done in the great spirit that they will later be done in.

You haven't even begun. You must pause first, the way one must always pause before a great spirit, if only to take a good breath.

Happy old age is coming on bare feet, bringing with it grace and gentle words, and ways that grim youth has never known.

LULLABY

I did not attend my first concert of classical music until I was eighteen. The concert was in a small chapel high in the Swiss Alps, and there were so many people packed in under that roof it felt claustrophobic, but at least I had a bench to sit on—I suppose you'd call it a pew. After about fifteen minutes of listening to the music I fell asleep. I wasn't bored, I was relaxed, and, I suppose, happy (I've never been able to figure out how happiness feels). When the concert was over I woke up and was embarrassed to have been sleeping. The audience was on its way out. Have you ever noticed how after a performance the floor is littered with programs? An hour before, when the concert began, everyone wanted their program, everyone held their program with both hands and would not dream of letting it go, but afterwards people leave them on the empty seats, where they slip quietly to the floor. That has always made me sad. And so on my way out I picked up one of the abandoned programs from the floor. *Brahms's Lullabies*—that was the whole concert! Suddenly I felt that perhaps by falling asleep I was the only one who had truly *heard* the music! Of course I felt this to make myself feel better—feelings are strange that way. Brahms's lullabies. I slipped the program into my bag, as a memento of a lovely nap, and left the chapel. Outside it was cold and so starry that I stood there for a while looking up. Of that night, I remember the stars more than the music, but I remember that while looking up at the stars I was thinking of the programs scattered on the floor. I can't say that Brahms is one of my favorite composers, but one artist I have always loved is Giacometti, the Swiss sculptor and painter; when I look at his work I can see the tension everyone talks about, yet his work has always made me extraordinarily calm, as Brahms did that evening: as if everything, stretched out in infinite silence and space, were part of this big drawing, and his drawings were part of this big drawing, which was so big that to see the whole thing would put anyone to sleep—I mean you would lose consciousness. Giacometti, my lullaby. Henry Miller is another artist who can put you to sleep. I often fall asleep while reading him. When he uses that hard word *cunt* again and again, it finally becomes something soft, so very soft, which is startling because a cunt really *is* soft, it's a warm, soft, wet-while-young place, a *spot* really, given the size of the universe, the way a star is a spot, but there are so many of them—I mean cunts—who can keep track? Henry Miller himself has pointed this out, and so Henry Miller becomes bored and disenchanted and excited at the same time, and that is an interesting thing; if you want to go to sleep but the lullaby *excites* you, what can you do, I mean really, what can you do? You can listen to Brahms, you can look at Giacometti, you can read Henry Miller, but each will tell you in his own way that there is nothing, absolutely nothing, but the stars looking down on you, even when you think you are looking up. How heavy-handed I feel just writing this, how heavy my hand feels, how heavy my eyes, my very hair is dragging me down, but it is a truth and if you sleep through a truth you will but wake at the bitter end.

TAKE FRANK

Take Frank. Frank is a bright boy, yet a lazy and stubborn high school student, one who holds in disdain all of his teachers, especially the dedicated, passionate ones. All of his English teachers, since at least the seventh grade, have been passionate. They have all told Frank that if he would only read this or that book he would fall in love with it, he would find himself hidden between its pages, he would have his "mind blown away." Frank does not like the idea of having his mind blown away, he finds it suicidal; Frank likes his mind the way it is and he intends to keep it. Frank does not want to fall in love, nor to see himself or find himself, he sees himself every day and he finds himself fine, he is exactly who he is and wants to be. He does not understand what all the fuss is about. So when Mr. Pacquette, his English teacher, approached Frank and offered a way for Frank to make up his missing credit, Frank was not even vaguely interested. In Frank's view, things existed or did not exist, and things that did not exist could not be said to be missing; he lacked a certain amount of credit, that was a fact, but the credit had not gone missing, it simply did not exist. Why go looking for something that did not exist? His nonexistent credit was not a teenager who had been abducted, or was lost in the woods, there was no picture of it that could be nailed near the bus stop, it was not a cat, he did not care or have feelings for this thing that was, supposedly, missing. He, himself, had no sense of loss, it was Mr. Pacquette who had a sense of loss; passionate people, Frank had observed, had above all else a sense of loss. He knew this was somehow connected to their enthusiasm, their hysterical insistence, their waving about of their arms. Mr.

Pacquette did in fact wave his arms about when he told Frank that he had found "the perfect assignment," that all Frank had to do was read Herman Melville's short story "Bartleby, the Scrivener" and write a short paper on it, and all the missing credit would be restored, while at the same time Frank's mind would be blown away—apparently this was a bonus. Frank was not interested and said so, he said "I would prefer not to," which Mr. Pacquette recognized instantly as the famous, and only, words of Bartleby the scrivener, though Frank did not recognize them as belonging to anyone other than himself, they were his own words, they had just left his mouth hadn't they? Yet Frank's words only caused Mr. Pacquette to wave his arms more wildly, and Frank could see his teacher was on the verge of having a *point*, another thing Frank couldn't care less about and did not want to be privy to. So when Mr. Pacquette began to get even more excited, when he opened his mouth more widely than was humanly necessary and said "That's just the *point*!" Frank said "I'd prefer not to" and left the room. Which left the passionate English teacher alone in sad thought, thinking of all the missed connections and opportunities in life, of all the failures. He felt sorry for Frank, and for Herman Melville, and for Bartleby, and for himself; he felt sorry for the sad fate of literature, which should be able to save the world but can't, through no fault of its own. Meanwhile Frank was walking home along the railroad tracks, the sun shone down on him, his mind was intact, he was doing exactly what he wanted to be doing, he was in his own world, free, not trapped between the pages of a book, and if he saw an insect he could squash it under his foot, or he could save it in a matchbox he carried in his pocket for that purpose.

RECOLLECTIONS OF MY CHRISTMAS TREE

I have always been vulnerable when confronted with Christmas decorations, and I am sitting in my living room staring at them. The lights on the tree are blinking on and off and I'm mesmerized. I have never been to a hypnotist but maybe mesmerization is the last state you enter before going over the edge into hypnosis. Maybe being mesmerized is the last thing you remember. It does seem to be a state all its own. When I was a child I did the same thing—watched the lights blink on and off, alone in the living room at night. The only difference is I know a lot more about Christmas now than I did then. I knew practically nothing then. My mother put an electric candle in each window, they were ivory-colored plastic, and at the end of each taper, near the bulb, fake drips of wax were molded; I loved the drips the most, it meant that the candles looked real to people inside the house, not just to people looking at them from the outside. What I didn't know then was that these decorations evolved from the Jewish menorah, the Hebrew festival of lights. I don't think my mother knew that either, but if she did she never mentioned it. And I certainly never contemplated the resemblance of a sleigh to a cradle. A sleigh is basically a very large cradle. The runners of the sleigh are what makes the cradle rock. Once there was a very eccentric man, in the nineteenth century in upstate New York, and when he was in his fifties he had a carpenter build him a cradle. I saw it in a museum, the biggest cradle ever made, and every night he slept in it, and when he entered his last illness he stayed in the cradle day and night, feeling the sensual throes of the cradle while somebody nursed and rocked him. I mean in the sense of caring for him. He died in his cradle, and the card on the wall of the museum said he was happy at the end. When I was a child one of my ornaments was a little red velveteen sleigh. I used to put a tiny doll in it, but now it is empty. I don't even like it anymore and when I was decorating the tree I thought about throwing it away but then I remembered the man in the cradle and decided to keep it. My mother and father also decorated the outside of our house with lights. We lived in a different house every year, so it wasn't easy—the length of the light strings kept changing. People who live in the same house every year don't think about things like that, their dimensions stay the same, there's no need to adjust anything, ever. After the lights were up on the outside of the house, my father would put us in the car and drive around the neighborhood, looking at the lights on the other houses. Sometimes he made disparaging remarks and sometimes in silence admired them. When he admired them he would make changes in his own lights the following year, but as we were by then in a new house none of the neighbors knew we were copycats. The most beautiful yard we ever saw had a snow scene with a frozen pond in the middle and life-sized figure skaters who floated across the pond wearing muffs. This was in Southern California, so everything was fake—the snow, the frozen pond, even the skaters were fake, and when they moved you could hear a slight whir under the ice—I guess it came from a motor. My father couldn't copy that—I could tell from his face that he was defeated. In those days everyone had lights. Not a single house was without them. That's one thing that has certainly changed. Today, only poor people have lights, and the poorest people of all have the most of them. At least this is true of the town I live in. There is one street that has the poorest people of all and at Christmas it is ablaze with lights, there are electric deer on the lawns and huge inflatable Santas, the roofs have more Santas descending in sleighs with reindeer, that kind of thing. The rich people think it is ugly, they don't bother anymore and they worry about the electric bill. They try to live calm, natural lives. They bake all their own bread, they make cookies and cakes and pies from scratch, they make their own beer and their own wine and liquors and they grow their own food in the summer—and come winter, when they want a Christmas tree or some holly, they just walk out on their land and cut it. Poor people have to use money, they have to go to the store and buy food, especially the kind that is already made. It didn't used to be that way. When I was a kid, it was understood that poor people had to make everything themselves while rich people got to buy things. My mother bought whole cakes at the grocery store and said we were lucky, not to have to make them ourselves. Now everything is reversed. If my mother and father were still alive they would be very confused. I think we would all become confused, eventually, if we didn't die. Maybe death prevents a major confusion that would, if it were allowed to go on, eventually kill us all. When I was little, one Christmas ritual majorly confused me. My mother had a little ceramic sleigh that sat on the table. It was driven by a ceramic Santa and pulled by ceramic reindeer. Every year I had to wrap empty matchboxes so they looked like tiny presents. Then we piled them in the sleigh; they were the presents Santa was hauling. But they were empty, and it made me sad. My mother would sit at the table smoking, watching me wrap the matchboxes. Can't we put anything in them? I asked. No, she said, they're fake. Couldn't we pretend? I said. That's what we're doing, she said. I mean *real pretend*, I said, but she just stared off into space and I knew the conversation had ended. One thing is for certain—I wouldn't want to be a Christmas tree. It would be nice to be the center of attention, to be so decorated and lit that people stared at you in wonder, and made a fuss over you, and were mesmerized. That would be nice. But then you'd start dropping your needles and people would become bored with you and say you weren't looking so good, and then they'd take off all your jewelry, and haul you off to the curb where you would be picked up and crushed and eventually burned. That's the terrible part. Maybe that's why so many people today have fake trees. They are quite popular. Their limbs come apart and you can put them in boxes and store them. You can have one of these trees until you die and you can pass it on to your children. They may not be real but when you look at them you can't tell the difference. That always makes people happy—not being able to tell the difference. And happiness, to want to be happy, is the most natural thing of all. That man in his big cradle was happy, though I never understood why, when he died, they didn't just saw the runners off and use it as his coffin. I don't think anyone would have noticed; in the end, the difference between a cradle and a coffin is hardly worth mentioning, though then again I wouldn't have seen the cradle later, in the museum, and if that hadn't happened I wouldn't have kept my red velveteen sleigh, I would have just thrown it away. No, never! When it comes to Christmas, when Christmas comes, I sit firmly on the lap of Charles Dickens, and repeat after him: Welcome, Everything! At this well-remembered time, when Everything is capable, with the greatest of ease, of being changed into Anything. On this day we shut out Nothing!

Purple sadness is the sadness of classical music and egg-plant, the stroke of midnight, human organs, ports cut off for part of every year, words with too many meanings, in-cense, insomnia, and the crescent moon. It is the sadness of play money, and icebergs seen from a canoe. It is possi-ble to dance to purple sadness, though slowly, as slowly as it takes to dig a pit to hold a sleeping giant. Purple sadness is pervasive, and goes deeper into the interior than the world's greatest nickel deposits, or any other sadness on earth. It is the sadness of depositories, and heels echoing down a long corridor, it is the sound of your mother clos-ing the door at night, leaving you alone.

Black sadness is the ashling, its remains are scattered over several provinces, it is the sadness of rakes and hyphenated names, of clouds who think they are grapes, it is the sadness of brooches, which may be worn on the breast or at the neck but how sad none see the sadness of detail there, the woman playing a guitar without strings, the hare leaping from the fox in vain, it is sadness torn and sadness rent, it is the hole in sadness from which no words escape and no soul can spring, it is the calorific sadness of bombs. Many of us used to own a black velvet skirt. It is little Angie Moss on her way to the fair, it is there she will have her first adventure.

ONE GIRL'S THEORY

Mr. Timothy Wells was killed in an instant by fallen timber at the raising of a large barn, 18th October, a clear day, no tuft in our sky. For Thy information he was 28 years of age and after the accident his eyes remained open. After reading that, I had to leave the graveyard. How you bait your hooks is immoral. I didn't want to think about it so I stopped for lunch in a joint off the lake and was seated in a booth next to the window. The window had lace curtains, the curtains had acorns and oak leaves woven into them. I was served a glass of water, one bowl of pea soup, and a pair of saltines packaged together. Two people in the next booth were talking. Billions and billions of years in the future, said one. Billions and billions of years ago, said the other. It made me sad so I left, leaving the saltine packaging next to a nifty tip. What were those people talking about? Once I imagined a baby born with eight or nine hearts on a planet with as many moons, but that wasn't nearly enough. Fishing boats bobbed along the edges of the lake. There didn't seem to be anyone listening to them. Once in Thy wisdom (a long time ago, in England) you caused a baby to be born without a brain. It lived a few days then the doctors lit into it, that's when they found the empty space in its skull. None believe this true story, their brains won't let them. But I think this babe was your love child, and everyone who reads about him, you kill.

TO A MAGAZINE

I am rejecting your request for a letter of rejection. One must reject everything in order to live. That may be true, but the rejected know another knowledge—that if they were not rejected, heaven would descend upon the earth in earthly dreams and an infinite flowering of all living forms would form a silveresque film over our sordid history, which has adventitiously progressed through violent upheavals in reaction to rejection; without rejection there would be no as-we-know-it earth. What is our ball but a rejected stone flung from the mother lode? The rejected know that if they were nonrejected a clear cerulean blue would be the result, an endless love ever dissolving in more endless love. This is their secret, and none share it save them. They remain, therefore, the unbelieved, they remain the embodiment of heaven herself. Let others perpetuate life as we know it—that admixture, that amalgam, the happy, the sad, the profusion of all things under the sunny moon existing in a delicate balance, such as it is. Alone, the rejected walk a straight path, they enter a straight gate, they see in their dreams what no one else can see—an end to all confusion, an end to all suffering, an elysian mist of eternally good vapor. Forgive me if I have put your thoughts into words. It was the least I could do for such a comrade, whose orphaned sighs reach me in my squat hut.

MILKSHAKE

I am never lonely, and never bored. Except when I bore myself, which is my definition of loneliness—to bore oneself. It makes a body lonesome, that. Today I am very bored, and very lonely. I can think of nothing better to do than grind salt and pepper into my milkshake, which I have been doing since I was thirteen, which was so long ago the very word *thirteen* has an old-fashioned ring to it, one might as well say "Ottoman Empire." Traditionally, thirteen is an unlucky number. Little did I know at thirteen that I was on the road, by a single action, to loneliness and boredom. My friend Vicki and I were sitting at the lunch counter in Woolworth's, waiting for the milkshakes we had ordered—hers chocolate, mine vanilla—when she got up to go to the ladies' room. The chocolate shake came while she was gone and as a joke I sprinkled salt and pepper on it, because I was, though I didn't know it, young and callous and cruel. Vicki came back, she took the paper off her straw, she stuck her straw in her milkshake, she sucked through the straw for what seemed an eternity, and then she swallowed, which seemed like forever. *This is the best milkshake I have ever had.* That's what she said, though she didn't say it as much as she sighed it. *The best shake I've ever had.* In such sudden and unexpected ways does boredom begin. I tried her milkshake, I told her what I had done, the vanilla shake came and we salt-and-peppered that one, too, and afterwards we were bored, so we went shopping—we were in Woolworth's after all—though by shopping we meant shoplifting, as any lonely bored thirteen-year-old knows. Vicki stole a little tub of the latest invention, lip gloss, which was petroleum jelly dyed pink, and I stole a yellow lace mantilla to wear to Mass on Easter Sunday, though I never wore it to Mass: I wore it to confession the Saturday before, confessing to the priest that I had stolen the very thing I was wearing on my head. Why not? I had nothing else to confess. Playing a mean trick on my best friend, even one that turned out all right, didn't seem worth the bother. What bothered me was that the priest seemed bored by my confession; I had thought to shock him, but it was he who shocked me, as I had so little experience of adult boredom. He gave me three Hail Marys and closed the screen. What was happening? I had shocked myself by stealing the mantilla and then confessing it, but bored the priest, whose boredom now shocked me, though it would bore me later, years later, when lip gloss was as common as clover, when the idea of Catholic women covering their heads was antiquated, when priests were suspected of being callous and cruel, and the combination of salt and sugar was a raging trend, served in all the swank joints and upscale places. But, as I said, I am never lonely and never bored, and if today is an exception, it is the age-old exception of every day, for every day turns into tomorrow, and tomorrow turns into today, and today into yesterday, and I confess there is very little any of us can do to change it.

Gray sadness is the sadness of paper clips and rubber bands, of rain and squirrels and chewing gum, ointments and unguents and movie theaters. Gray sadness is the most common of all sadnesses, it is the sadness of sand in the desert and sand on the beach, the sadness of keys in a pocket, cans on a shelf, hair in a comb, dry-cleaning, and raisins. Gray sadness is beautiful, but not to be confused with the beauty of blue sadness, which is irreplaceable. Sad to say, gray sadness is replaceable, it can be replaced daily, it is the sadness of a melting snowman in a snowstorm.

Red sadness is the secret one. Red sadness never appears sad, it appears as Nijinsky bolting across the stage in mid-air, it appears in flashes of passion, anger, fear, inspiration, and courage, in dark unsellable visions; it is an upside-down penny concealed beneath a tea cozy, the even-tempered and steady-minded are not exempt from it, and a curator once attached this tag to it: *Because of the fragile nature of the pouch no attempt has been made to extract the note.*

AMONG THE CLOUDS

That was the summer there were so many clouds we didn't know what to do with them. They overflowed the sky—they were on our streets, in our homes, in our drawers, and in our cabinets. They were in our cars and on our buses, I even saw them in taxis. No one had ever seen so many clouds, to the extent that, as often happens with a glut, no one could remember a time without them. Our legislators tried to ship them to another country, but the question came back—what would one do with so many clouds? There was no wind, no rain, nothing to break them up or break off the endless building up of them. Ship them to Mars, someone said; but Mars could not sustain them. You needed an atmosphere for that, and how odd was that, since so many clouds clouded our atmosphere and every citizen felt they were in a play, at the theater, overcome by another's mood, at the mercy of the infinite nostalgia of subconscious dictates. I was not the first to be surprised and often terrified by their images. They cast long shadows in an unearthly light. Some were blue, some were gray, some black, some white, some were pink, some were lavender, some orange, some a ghastly purple. All cast a trance and a silence upon us. I registered without choice the complaints of a multitude. Our dreams of a solution, even the most obscure, dissolved in the profound and vital roots of an intractable reality. The picture of a limp cloud watching us was undeniable. They were irrational, impossible, baffling and alarming, solitary, in strata, stippled as a fish's back, fantastically shaped, and plain as the day is long. They hypnotized us and paralyzed us. Yet they remained, in the highest and lowest places, and the meticulous exact realism of them convinced us to capture them, and zoo them, and feed them, to the extent others, far into the researchable future, would be able to see what was the temporary but encroaching weight of their total reality, and perhaps understand our hopelessness of ever understanding them, why they were so crowded among us, given we were crowned with brains to override them, which proved impossible, though there are so few left who remember. Even now, so many years later, when strolling idly, say on a Sunday, under a spotless sky, when I meet a child carrying in her right hand, like a torch, a tuft of spun sugar on a stick, the familiar cry of that summer comes back to me, the one that floated out of the mouths of so many children: *O Mother, O Father, wherefore art thou? I cannot see to find thee among so many clouds.*

MY PRIVATE PROPERTY

It is sad, is it not, that no one today displays any interest in the art of shrunken heads. Men, women, and children walk on streets, they cross fields and enter forests, they run along the edges of oceans, but none of them, to the best of my knowledge, are thinking about shrunken heads. I am thinking about shrunken heads, but keep the thought to myself, that is, inside my head, for if the subject is raised at all, it is met with horror, on account of the violence involved in the necessary removal of the head before you can shrink it. But as an art and a conception, the tribes of the Amazon displayed a genius that deserves our awe; miniaturizing and preserving a human head is a glory and wonder on the scale of the Great Pyramids. I recently encountered a passage on shrunken heads in *Kon-Tiki*, the best-selling account by Thor Heyerdahl of his journey, with five companions, on a simple wooden raft that set sail from the coast of Peru in 1947 and landed on an uninhabited South Sea island 101 days later. The journey, which even professional mariners thought would end in disaster, was undertaken to prove Heyerdahl's theory that Polynesia was settled by peoples of the South American continent. It is not a book that is much read today, but the copy I found at the Goodwill was in its 21st printing in 1962, so it is fair to think that for many years people did think about shrunken heads, which are mentioned in passing on page 62. By 1947, when Heyerdahl and his men were building their raft in a naval yard in Lima, the market for shrunken heads was strictly an illegal one, but there were still people who made their living selling the desiccated top portion of the human body. The Amazonian jungle is very dense and such a thing is hard to control. Heyerdahl's account is brief and sketchy but one learns that it is done like this: after the requisite decapitation, the skull is smashed and removed through the neck, leaving the skin of the head intact, like a sack of flesh, which is then filled with hot sand, which causes the sack to shrink without losing its shape or any of its features. The shrunken head is about the size of an orange. One of Thor's men, who had lived in the jungle a long time, had a friend who was murdered and whose head was shrunk; a promise was made to spare the murderers in exchange for the head, and so the little head was eventually handed to its widow, who fainted. Thereafter it was kept in a trunk where it mildewed and from time to time had to be hung by its hair on a clothesline and left in the air to dry. Every time its widow saw it, she fainted. One day a mouse got into the trunk and that was the end of the head. To be eaten by a mouse! To be eaten by worms is charmless and inevitable. But for your head to be nibbled at by a mouse, for your head to become a bit of moldy cheese on a plate—that was something that spoke volumes about reversals of power, about foolishness and vanity. It reminded me of a nineteenth-century Japanese drawing I had once seen—*Mice Transcribing a Book*, by Kawanabe Kyōsai—in which red-eyed white mice wearing kimonos are kneeling at a low desk transcribing a book, while off in the corner naked black mice are devouring the pages of a previously transcribed book. Am I vain to think of my head as a book? Am I not transcribing the book of my head as I write? To be eaten by a mouse! I had to learn more, so I did some research and found a more detailed account of how it is done, a method used by the Jivaro of the Ecuadoran and Peruvian Amazon, who, as far as I can tell, are known today as the Shuar; these ethnocentricities become amazingly complicated. The Jivaro, or Shuar, slit the head-flesh up the back to remove the skull, throwing the skull in the river to appease the river gods. The eyes and the mouth are sewn shut, to paralyze the spirit, which, having died violently, would be bent on revenge. The flesh-head is boiled for two hours until the skin is dark and rubbery and one-third its original size. The skin is then turned inside out and any flesh still sticking to the inside is scraped off, then the head is inverted back and by this time resembles an empty rubber glove. The final shrinking is done with sand, and hot stones dropped one at a time through the neck opening, constantly rotated inside to prevent scorching. The sand enters the places the stones cannot, the crevices of the nose and ears, and hot stones are applied to the exterior, too, to seal and shape the features. Surplus hair is singed off and the finished product hung over a fire to harden and blacken. A heated machete is applied to the lips to dry them, and then they are lashed together with native fiber. The word for shrunken heads is *tsantsa* (pronounced *san-sah*), and the process has been in existence for as long as anyone can remember, an art so old it has no known origin. It takes about a week to shrink a head, the artist working daily. A ceremony follows where a string is inserted in the head so it can be worn around the neck, for the head of the enemy is a trophy, a living trophy of sorts, for it contains the spirit of the vanquished. Some tribes, though, didn't keep the heads after the ceremony but fed them to animals or gave them to children as a plaything to be lost. In this instance, they are dolls, but with a difference—they are *real* dolls, every girl's dream. It is hard to fake a shrunken head, but once they became a commodity—enter the white man—many tried. Some clever folk used other animals altogether, such as the heads of monkeys and goats.

Where there is value, there will be experts, and experts say that nose hair and ears are especially hard to fake. An expert examining a shrunken head to determine whether or not it is *real* is not unlike an art expert examining a supposed Rembrandt to determine whether or not it is *real*: magnifying glasses are used. But I keep thinking about the mouse, who didn't care or know whether the head was anything other than a real meal. We eat jerky don't we? Most of all, I like the idea that a head can continue to have a fate after it's dead. And the story of the widow who fainted every time she saw her husband's head on the clothesline took me back to my own first encounter with a shrunken head. When I was sixteen years old and in school in Brussels I would very often play hooky, skipping school it is also called, and always when I did I did the same thing, I took a tram to the outskirts of the city and wandered through that marble mausoleum commonly called the Congo Museum. I may not have been a writer at sixteen, but I was most emphatically a daydreamer, and felt deliriously happy to be free, wandering under the hanging canoes, staring at the stuffed elephants and peering into the eyeholes of masks, with which I felt a special relationship. Of course I am filled with retrospective shame, but not for my feeling of freedom, freedom is something one should never feel ashamed of, but for my sheer and utter ignorance; I can now say that my ignorance was not in any way caused by my absence from the classroom, I can assure you my school did not teach what I now know to be true—that the museum I wandered in was built on rape and plunder and pillage and oppression and murder, that everything in it was stolen, that the very wealth necessary for such acquisition was stolen, wealth acquired by force of so filthy and unspeakable an evil our heads cannot fathom it and have no single word for it, but must resort to endless corridors of words, each corridor turning into another corridor a thousand miles longer than the last in our hopeless search for some inner chamber of understanding that does not exist. Among these millions of words time passes, and in time slavery passes, if only on paper, a page shuffled among thousands of pages, and then there are two words, *rubber* and *ivory*, that break off from the others and river around the world in the forms of automobile tires and piano keys. But commerce and culture quickly take us down a corridor leading to more automobile tires and more piano keys, and their equivalent—money—and I want to go the way of shrunken heads, and dolls, soft rubbery flesh and ivory-like porcelain, skin and bones, faces and masks. At sixteen, I was not much the other side of dolldom, so it is little wonder that there in the Congo Museum I fell in love with a shrunken head. Of course, the head was not Amazonian but African. I don't know how the art evolved on that continent, but genius flourishes everywhere, it has always been so and will always be so, and there will always be people who believe otherwise. As I said, a shrunken head is as close to a *real* doll as one could ever come, and in this sense it is both a child's toy and an adult toy—it's another person after all—and I was not then, nor am I now, immune to the charms of having someone else to play with. He was dangling from an invisible thread, much as a spider does, from the top of a glass case taller than I was. He *was* the size of an orange. He was particular and unique and human and utterly real, a man with eyes and eyelashes and hair (apparently the Africans do not close the eyes of their dolls). It was only later that I learned that the hair and eyelashes do not shrink with the flesh of the face, and so the shrunken often have the luxurious eyelashes of a child, and the hair is much longer than the face, though often cut, so great is the human impulse toward proportion. But my man had long, uncut hair, and as it was 1969 I didn't think anything of it; all the men I liked had long, uncut hair. His skin had the sheen of an eggplant—it must have been oiled—and all the purples of that fruit were in it; his nose was broad and flat, his eyes deeply set, unnaturally so, and beautifully shining, but so many years have passed I cannot be sure of what was there and what was not, though I returned to look at him countless times; he was, after a while, what I came to look at, and at some point I began to commune with him. Yes, I gave life to an inanimate object, but can a human head ever really be said to be an inanimate object? He was not a skull, he was not decomposing, he was not mangled in any way. He had been, and *was*, a person. I don't remember what it was we communed about, but he possessed me as I possessed him, and to possess the head of a beloved, no less than the head of an enemy, is the greatest sickness on earth. I could enter the museum blindfolded and turn exactly the right corners, one after another, to find myself standing before him at eye-level. I shall never forget his expression: he looked *startled*. No other words come to mind. And though I could not see myself, I must have looked startled, too. We stood facing each other the way, when you come upon a deer unexpectedly, you both freeze for a moment, mutually startled, and in that exchange there seems to be but one glance, as if you and the other are sharing the same pair of eyes. The years passed. I left the city, I never returned, the signage in the museum changed, of that I am sure, but the impression left upon me by the shrunken head has never changed, so that I now wonder why human beings do not incorporate the art of shrinking heads into their burial rites. I am serious. What prevents us from saving the heads of the dead we bury, since we can make them the size of oranges (or apples), and keeping them, out of the deepest love and respect, for our descendants, for whom the heads will become ancestors, for what are ancestors but *the loved ones of our loved ones*, since a single act of love, down through the ages, has procured what we call the future? I am presuming, of course, that procreation involves love, which it very often does not, and so I hesitate to say love is the greatest traveler, I could just as easily say sex; perhaps love is but symbolic behavior toward sex—it is certainly symbolic behavior toward the living and the dead. I am most interested in shrunken heads as symbolic behavior toward the dead. Marks of being a human involve symbolic behavior toward the dead; no other animal does it to the extent humans do. Don't we carry photographs of the heads of those we love who have died? Don't we frame their heads and keep them on the mantel as reminders of all that is precious and binds us to this life? And before there were photographs, that rage of the well-to-do, that sign of commerce and culture, there were hand-painted miniatures (if you could afford them), exquisitely detailed renditions of the head, kept in a protective locket or box that could be carried inside a jacket or coat. Someone leaving on a long journey would carry such a head. A Belgian officer or intrepid explorer would carry such a head into the African jungle. Surely Commandant Dhanis (afterwards Baron), making his way toward Katanga, carried such a head, and surely from time to time he took it out of his coat or jacket and looked at it. And his heart was filled with love, even if that love did not extend to the foliage around him, nor to the people whose habitat it was, several of whom were artists in shrinking heads, no less than the miniaturist. The human heart is hard to fathom, no less than the human head. They both contribute to human behavior, the hardest of all to fathom. I don't know when psychiatrists and psychologists were first called *shrinks*, but the term has stuck. I confess I don't understand it myself, for my personal experience with psychotherapy is that it expands the head in wondrous ways, it educates the mind to view itself, and others, from new perspectives amounting to vistas. There is nothing small about it. I first began seeing a shrink after the death of my mother. I was then in my mid-forties and considered myself highly intelligent. A large part of my intelligence depended on my total ignorance of how ignorant I really was. I was not unlike Commandant Dhanis, the Belgian aristocrat who carried a miniature head into the jungle without realizing the Congolese were far superior in that art. Even today, when I muse about preserving the heads of loved ones by postmortem shrinkage, I am ignorant; I seldom stop to consider the obstacles and absurdities of my plan. My mother's head, for example, could not have been shrunk by any means, as she died from injuries sustained in a gruesome accident, which resulted in her head, during the few remaining weeks of her life, swelling to inhuman proportions. My mother's head went, rather quickly, from the size of a head to the size of a watermelon to the size of a prizewinning pumpkin. It was impossible to look at it (her) unless you pretended you were watching a horror film and that it wasn't real, but was a giant grotesque doll created by special effects. At least that is how I remember enduring one such viewing. Unlike a shrunken head, when a human head is enlarged it cannot sustain its features, the eyes and the nose and the mouth all disappear in one gigantic gelatinous mass; such a head does not remotely resemble the person it belongs to. So much so, I pinned a photograph of my mother over her hospital bed so that the doctors and nurses might know what their patient looked like. It seems strange to me now, the gesture of that photograph, as none of the medical staff knew her before her accident, and there was no hope at any time that her head would deflate to recognizable proportions. I think I pinned that photograph up for myself, so I could remember her as I knew her. No, my mother's head, sadly, could not have been shrunk, by even the greatest artist, and yet her head has always figured into my daydream of having twelve shrunken heads, each one belonging to someone who has passed through my life, touching me in deep and unforgettable ways, and I would keep my dozen heads in an egg carton made especially for them, twelve beloved heads kept safe and together. I would never let them mold or rot, I would not let the mice near them, their fate would be to remain exactly as they were in life, exactly as they *are*, albeit orange-sized and portable, and from time to time I would take them out and look at them and be startled, and I think of the widow who fainted at the sight of her husband's head, and I think if I could hold the head of a single beloved in my hand I would indeed feel faint, but I think also I would get used to it, I would grow calm and be moved in the tenderest of ways, just the sight of them there in my hand, resting gently and safely (a shrunken head cannot be broken) with such tiny and shining eyes, why, resting gently and safely with such tiny and shining eyes it would be as if they were but babies, returning to live again, and I could touch their faces. I am ashamed to think of the baby heads as my private property, but I do. It has been said that inside the human head is to be found the only freedom that exists for all, but very often that freedom grows lonely and bored and frightened and yearns to join another head, very often owning one head is not enough, owning your own head gives rise to the desire for the head of another, out of the perfectly natural desire for love and communion. But out of greed, out of the desire for control and power, grows a monster, the desire to own as many heads as possible. None of us are immune—who doesn't want more clients, patients, customers, readers—but desire can swell to inhuman proportions. Thus the King of Belgium declared a vast territory as his private property, and all heads within it, including (unbeknownst to him) all the shrunken heads, heads shrunk after a week's worth of artful work. I don't really know anything about heads, though I spend a disproportionate amount of my time thinking about them, and more time than ever since seeing a shrink. I am not even sure I own my own head, but my innermost fantasy is to own twelve beloved heads nestled in an egg carton, to comfort me in moments of dearth in exchange for my infinite love. How can I call myself benevolent? I want, as my personal private property, twelve human heads. I have often thought God needs prayers to remind himself he is important, and still matters. Without our interceding glances, what would he be but a shrunken head on the end of a thread in a museum of ideas? Sometimes I think there is no place left for me to go but back to the Congo Museum, that horrific monument of smashed lies and beautiful things, and stand face-to-face before a face I can barely remember but do, and pray to that shriveled thing that when I die, as I must, let someone preserve me as I was then, that first day, ignorant, innocent, at my most beautiful, and overcome by another. It occurs to me I wanted to die that day. Why else would I have skipped school and wandered off alone and found a friend among the dead? One who thrilled me to life? O my pantheon of shrunken heads, struck like new-laid eggs in a carton, comfort me when my rivers are high, comfort me when my waters are gone, for I can almost hear you breathing.

OLD IMMORTALITY

The Earl of Staffordshire was the least eccentric of his ancestral line; one of his forebears had died after eating horse manure in the belief it would cure him of jealousy, a belief we cannot deny proved true in the end. The present Earl had no intention of dying, he sought in its place the immortality of art, specifically that of the writer, specifically that of his rival, Sir Walter Scott, whose Waverley novels were being read by everyone in the shire who could read. Their anonymity had long been dispelled, the year was 1815, and the Earl of Staffordshire, of whom we speak, set out to write a sequel to his favorite, *Old Mortality*, and gave his book the title *Old Immortality* without having yet written a single word. But write he did, by day and by night, behind heavy curtains, by the light of six tapers, and with a curious nib at the end of his quill, a gold nib specially made from his wife's golden wedding ring, she having died in childbirth along with his heir some thirty years previous. The Earl found he could not quite sustain the life of a novelist and the novel ended after only eighty pages, and of the tale we shall only say that its greatest merit was how profoundly it illustrated the old adage *It is a long lane that has no turning*. The Earl was nonetheless satisfied he had by his own hand acquired immortality, or if he had his doubts, they were as heavily curtained as his chambers. We would not be writing his story, even as simply and briefly as we mean to state it, if in fact he had not attained what he sought, though not quite in the manner of his original vision. Our Earl could have paid any price in England to ensure his book saw print, but hit upon a plan whose novelty became legend, giving *Old Immortality* its place in the cupboard of letters. He took the manuscript to the Staffordshire pottery, whose reputation, even at that time, was renowned among English potters, if not unsurpassed, and whose original wares reside today in museums the world over, and in the private collections of those individuals whose pressing passion is the historical significance of clay. The extra expense of securing the services of the pottery's master modeler, John Hackwood, was to our Earl equivalent to the effort of waving away a summer fly landed on the edge of his teacup. The plan was simple: one hundred four dining plates, bearing in sequence the text of his novel, including the title pages, author's preface, and an exquisite *finis* sheet embellished with garlands of eglantine, a last-minute inspiration designed to follow the page bearing the word *end*. Each plate was of bisque, a vitreous clay with a matte finish, and the color chosen was that of cream in the second hour of clotting. The plates were round, eleven inches in diameter with a slightly fluted edge but without a margin, in order to accommodate as many words as possible. On the underside was the mark of the pottery, the mark of the master modeler, John Hackwood, and a numeral designated to be both plate and page number. The text itself, modeled entirely by hand, in this case the hand of John Hackwood, was raised out of the bisque and given a jasper glaze, which in contrast to the bisque below provided easy readability. It is true the first sixty plates had to be destroyed, having been fired by an apprentice, but the Earl waved this expense off as if it were but the fly come back. *Old Immortality* took two days less than ten months to come to print, and the next step was for the Earl to present his book of plates to twenty-six esteemed guests invited to his table on the twenty-first of June 1816, for a seven-course banquet, the four central courses being reserved for the inaugural reading. The kitchen staff, in particular, spent the previous fortnight in rehearsal, for the guests were not to be simultaneously served, each guest being presented with food only after he had read his plate aloud to those assembled there for the occasion, and the food had to be kept hot behind the closed doors of the kitchen, and each footman, with perfect timing, fill each plate on the last breath of its recitation. Each guest needed to read four times, thus each guest needed to be presented with four different plates, set down at intervals as the evening, the meal, and the novel progressed. The Earl spared no expense, and provided his footmen with fresh gloves for each exchange of plates. It cannot be determined what was served that night, but we can imagine that after the soup bowls were cleared and the novel appeared, the quail came forth, the trout, the beef, the pastry filled with salmon, the Russian potatoes, the asparagus in aspic, all these and more perhaps, before the Earl held up his *finis* plate and the cheeses and pears and puddings were brought in. The wine flowed from start to finish, and if the chinatized literature did not go as smoothly, no one noticed, though it would perhaps be more accurate to record that no one spoke. What records we possess of the evening come down to us in the form of a review written by the Earl of Staffordshire before retiring to his bed that very night, though in his vigor he neglected the viands and detailed only the glorious reception of his immortal work, as indicated by the twenty-six stunned and speechless faces; though he did note the Duchess of Langford wore an offensively large jewel, though this doubtless harked back to his unsuccessful courtship of her some thirty years previous. The Earl gave his novel banquet twelve times a year until his death, never inviting the same guest twice, ensuring himself the readership he had dared dream of. And what became of the book? What became of the plates, the beautiful plates gleaming under the candelabra on the long table, one hundred four served in succession, twelve to a side, one at the head and one at the foot, each plate a page, each page exemplifying further it is a long lane that has no turning? Alas, the beautiful plates were destroyed by the Earl's grandnephew, who, in 1870, under the influence of the Arts and Crafts movement, invited his friends to a banquet that rapidly became debauched, and sometime after midnight while our Earl slept in his grave in the family chapel less than a mile removed, the youthful crew, who fancied themselves visionaries, and under the influence of wine and chloral hydrate, broke the plates one by one, flinging them against the fireplace after a cursory reading, which eventually ceased as the breaking went on, which is when they began to recite from memory recently published verses of Dante Gabriel Rossetti, verses the poet had buried with his first wife and just that past October exhumed from her coffin, leaving the lady poemless in her doom. O cold, cruel shards of Immortality! Not a single one remains to be unearthed by the garden wall. Yet one complete plate remains extant, with a single hairline crack crossing its bisque skull, if we can so call a plate whereon a man's mind is mapped; it is the one bordered with tangled vines of eglantine, that wild rose of poetic repute, and as you have guessed, dear reader, it bears the word *finis*.

Green sadness is sadness dressed for graduation, it is the sadness of June, of shiny toasters as they come out of their boxes, the table laid before a party, the smell of new strawberries and dripping roasts about to be devoured; it is the sadness of the unperceived and therefore never felt and seldom expressed, except on occasion by polka dancers and little girls who, in imitation of their grandmothers, decide who shall have their bunny when they die. Green sadness weighs no more than an unused handkerchief, it is the funereal silence of bones beneath the green carpet of evenly cut grass upon which the bride and groom walk in joy.

Pink sadness is the sadness of white anchovies. It is the sadness of deprivation, of going without, of having to swallow when your throat is no bigger than an acupuncture pin; it's the sadness of mushrooms born with heads too big for their bodies, the sadness of having the soles come off your only pair of shoes, or your favorite pair, it makes no difference, pink sadness cannot be measured by a gameshow host, it is the sadness of shame when you have done nothing wrong, pink sadness is not your fault, and though even the littlest twinge may cause it, it is the vast bushy top on the family tree of sadness, whose faraway roots resemble a colossal squid with eyes the size of soccer balls.

IN THE FOREST

When I wander in the forest I am drawn towards language, I see meaning is quaintly hidden, shooting up in dark wet woods, by roots of trees, old walls, among dead leaves, strangely lonely, suggestive of some wild individuality, silently symbolical of old Vienna, but lacking in details. When I wander in the forest, I am afraid of getting lost, and I feel most strongly that something is waiting for me, under a fallen log, behind a tree, there in some high-up hole in the tree trunk, though I seldom look up, no, as I walk I look down, drawn to the root system as I stumble, and I don't think that it is Sanskrit waiting for me, not for a minute, I think *what time is it* and *shouldn't I be getting home*, one can't always be wandering in meaning, dark as it is it will be getting darker, though if it begins to snow I look up, I lose myself in the snow as it falls between branches and builds up also on every one, I lose myself just as my steps are beginning to leave tracks in the snow on the forest floor, and soon the fallen logs are covered with snow, and when my tracks are covered I am completely lost, the snow has muffled everything, and the silence frightens me as much as the forest ever did.

THE HOODED DREAM OF DINING

Alice loved poetry. John loved poetry. Mary and Michael and Susan loved poetry. They went to a restaurant to sit together at a table and talk about the thing they loved. In walked David, who did not love poetry. He sat by himself at a small circular table, where he could hear other people talking but not what they were saying, and after he ordered he sat dreaming of mountaintops, of standing on a mountaintop looking down on the valley below, of watching a river snaking in the distance, of the wind in his hair. Still, being in a restaurant dreaming of mountaintops, he might as well have been fishing for pine needles. So David thought about his wife, who did not love poetry and did not love mountaintops, but loved red thread, which she collected for no reason and to no purpose. David thought of the time he stole a few strands from her desk and threw them in a stew he was making, to surprise her, but when he ladled the stew into her bowl and watched her eat it, it was apparent she didn't even notice. Still, a few hours later she seemed inexplicably happy, so he closed his eyes and thought of that.

LIKE A SCARF

For him, the affair was the flight of a weightless balloon borne by wind over a plaza. For her, the affair was the flight of a yellow silk scarf borne by the wind over the plaza, the rooftops of slanted tile, the highways, the beach, the rocky coastline and the inland forest; the scarf was thirty-three inches square with hand-rolled edges that had been rolled in Japan by the tiny fingers of Umi, a twenty-year-old worker in the silk district of Tomioka. Umi lived with her father, a widower, and after work in the factory returned home to care for him, preparing a meal of rice, eel, and radish, eating with him in silence, later burning incense in front of the household shrine, which contained a black-and-white photograph of her mother at the age of forty-two, a year before she died of cancer of the womb. Her last words had been spoken in a state of semiconsciousness, and it was unclear to whom they were addressed: *Let me.* The scarf whose edges Umi had rolled with her fingers was shipped to Milan to be sold in a department store, where it was bought by a man as a gift for his lover, who did not have the heart to tell him she never wore yellow (hadn't he noticed?) and the next day gave the scarf to her sister (who was delighted), telling her lover that the scarf had been blown off her head by a sudden gust of wind as she was crossing the plaza on her way to visit her sister, and though she was sorry to lose it, it had been the most beautiful sight (he should have been there), many heads tilted upwards to follow its path as it billowed across a cloudless lavender sky (he should have been there), it really was the most unexpected sight, one of the pedestrians even said out loud *Look, a balloon!* and later, at the dentist, the pedestrian described again that moment of grace, and the dentist listened very carefully as he injected Novocain into the man's gums, so carefully that later that evening he remembered to tell his wife about the flight of the balloon, which she instantly recognized because she had been there, she told her husband how she was crossing the plaza on her way to buy a pair of shoes when she saw it, a sight so beautiful she had wanted to take a video with her phone, but by the time she found her phone at the bottom of her bag the scarf was gone; still, the sight of the yellow silk scarf sailing over the plaza had so arrested her she no longer felt like buying shoes, and sat instead at a table at an outdoor café, ordering an aperitif of such a vivid color it appeared to be radioactive–Pernod, it was Pernod, how long had it been since either of them had had a Pernod, how many years, and could either of them remember?

Orange sadness is the sadness of anxiety and worry, it is the sadness of an orange balloon drifting over snow-capped mountains, the sadness of wild goats, the sadness of counting, as when one worries that another shipment of thoughts is about to enter the house, that a soufflé or Cessna will fall on the one day set aside to be unsad, it is the orange haze of a fox in the distance, it speaks the strange antlered language of phantoms and dead batteries, it is the sadness of all things left overnight in the oven and forgotten in the morning, and as such orange sadness becomes lost among us altogether, like its motive.

Yellow sadness is the surprise sadness. It is the sadness of naps and eggs, swan's down, sachet powder and moist towelettes. It is the citrus of sadness, and all things round and whole and dying like the sun possess this sadness, which is the sadness of the first place; it is the sadness of explosion and expansion, a blast furnace in Duluth that rises over the night skyline to fall reflected in the waters of Lake Superior, it is a superior joy and a superior sadness, that of revolving doors and turnstiles, it is the confusing sadness of the never-ending and the evanescent, it is the sadness of the jester in every pack of cards, the sadness of a poet pointing to a flower and saying *what is that* when what that is is a violet; yellow sadness is the ceiling fresco painted by Andrea Mantegna in the Castello di San Giorgio in Mantova, Italy, in the fifteenth century, wherein we look up to see we are being looked down upon, looked down upon in laughter and mirth, it is the sadness of that.

Autumn upset the young fox—in his anger and fear he went home crying bitterly with a dirty face and sweet violets still clasped unconsciously in his scratchy little hand. In his den, which was not snug, he put the violets in a mustard jar on the table, and ate a poor supper of half a young rabbit that had been killed so long ago it could rightfully be called old. He could not stop crying. He wished he could turn the pages of autumn the way he turned the pages of a book, which was, when he had come to the bottom, to stare at the page and say *Turn!* Turn, turn, turn, he cried in his evening stupor, in his despair. But nothing happened. The leaves kept falling, their colors changing even as they fell, turning this way and that, little staple holes of light in every one. The wind repeated its autumn song. Fox was so fearful of that song he went to bed without a pillow, lodging it under his door to keep the song out. In bed, calmer, he began his nighttime reading, a mystery, one whose hero was a forensic analyst working for the police, poring over forged documents, analyzing their handwriting, the make of pen used, the age and origin of the ink. A self-taught expert, the hero could infer from ink alone that a signature was actually written on September 23, and not the 16th, the date the letter was signed. He used microscopes, chemicals, and spectrographs. In tonight's chapter he was investigating the paper itself, its smudges and folds, the date of manufacture, fiber composition, color, texture, gloss, finish, length, width, thickness, weight, markings, and imperfections. Fox stopped at a singular sentence, his eyes narrowing in concentration: *Even a little staple hole may be the beacon which will light up the truth.* He read it again. Tears came out of their ducts and rolled down the sides of his face. He took his pillow from under the door, placed it under his head on the bed, and listening to the autumn song he fell asleep, having made peace with autumn, and the wild forest blood in his veins.

INKY FLOURISH

More than one hundred years after his death, it was found that a manuscript by Charles Baudelaire, upon close inspection, bore not just an inky flourish between poems the way today's poet might type an asterisk between paragraphs, but that each inky flourish was in fact a floating swan, an aquanaut of gracefully curving neck and carefully upturned tail feathers. And it was following this discovery that a later manuscript was examined, and upon closer inspection was clearly seen to contain not just an inky flourish between poems but floating cellphones, the starship *Enterprise*, and American hot dogs in white buns with a caterpillar of yellow mustard slinking lengthwise along the dog. *But none of these things had yet been invented!* was the cry of the critic. Ah, Charles Baudelaire, the visionary visionary, who once said *Paris may change; my melancholy is fast*, you have crawled from the depths of antiquity, by means of your own inky flourish, straight into the heart of our present-day turmoil. What say you now, Charlie?

PERSONALIA

When I was young, a fortune-teller told me that an old woman who wanted to die had accidentally become lodged in my body. Slowly, over time, and taking great care in following esoteric instructions, including lavender baths and the ritual burial of keys in the backyard, I rid myself of her presence. Now I am an old woman who wants to die and lodged inside me is a young woman dying to live; I work on her.

OUTCAST

If a poet who lived two hundred or twenty-one hundred years ago, say Catullus or Coleridge, sprang to life to read a poem written last year, and in it the poet said *I was stoned*, either would assume the poet was an outcast, his body covered with tiny potholes from all the rocks the villagers had thrown at him. There would be surprise that the stoned poet was even still alive, just as the poet would be astonished Catullus or Coleridge had sprung to life again, and if the ancient went to the poet's house for a visit and was offered a cold beer, and the light inside the refrigerator popped on, the ancient would drop dead all over again from a heart attack induced by the shock of electrical incomprehension. Well, that's how it is—the stars reach me, I see their light. Someone once explained to me that the stars are dead, but when I look up I don't act as if suddenly hit, I act normally, as if I understood everything, and I never think of how cold it is two hundred or twenty-one hundred miles out, nor do I think for a moment Catullus or Coleridge ever did, which means I think there is no difference between us, even if I have led you to believe there is.

TOWARDS A CAREFREE WORLD

Many of the most astonishing writers in the world had servants. It is doubtful they ever really washed the dishes. Which is too bad; I think they would have enjoyed washing the dishes, especially after dinner. Repetitive motion can take your mind off things. By *things* I mean the cares of this world. Repeated dish-washing can leave the hands chafed, but writers work also with their hands and often have, as a result of their work, a raised callus below the nail of the middle finger, formed by long contact and constant pressure between the flesh and the pen. It is doubtful Gustave Flaubert ever shoveled the snow in front of his home. It is interesting to imagine what his snow-shoveling style would have been, given the varying styles in which he wrote. Yet given the long hours of his working habits, we should not be surprised if his entire yard were emptied of snow. Shoveling takes your mind off things. Unless you are very troubled; in the case of the very troubled, no amount of shoveling snow or washing dishes will remove one's cares from the mind. Servants who did not own the land where the snow fell upon the house where the dishes were kept might have been very troubled. Money, illness, death, relations with others, including relatives: these are chief among our human woes; writers choose their subjects from among them. Long hours spent working on a novel, a story, a play, or a poem might also take one's mind off things. It seems strange, but possible, to use troubles to take your mind off of them. Perhaps the writer is a servant in his own way. I do not know who hires such servants, but the world seems full of them, ready for hire. If each household hired a writer-servant to sit and concentrate on the human troubles we each must bear, every household might be free from care. Yet it is hardly practical to hire a writer to sit in one's house all day, an extra room would be needed, and an extra servant hired to keep the children and animals quiet, so as not to disturb the writer, who, like all living things, must also be fed. And so the world has hit upon an ingenious plan involving books, which are relatively easy to bring into the house, take up but a small space, and never need to be fed: inside each book sits a servant with a callus on his finger, the author, who has concentrated on the cares of this world so that our minds may be free of them, as anyone knows who has ever sat for hours reading a book—the world seems far, far away, one forgets the time, one is surprised to look up and discover her own feet, which seem far, far away at that moment, or a potted plant on the other side of the room—where did it come from, how long has it been there? If a household employs servants to wash the dishes, shovel the snow, and water the plants, the reader is left doubly, even triply, carefree. But how odd, how very odd, that so many households containing a great many books, or a great many other things in any combination, are not exempt from care. In fact a great many cares find lodging there. It is deeply troubling to think that servants of any kind cannot fulfill their tasks to the extent we are left completely carefree. The servants need to work harder, or we need to have more of them; it is hard to know what to do, yet it seems obvious that something need be done.

SELF-CRITICISM

In a typical poem by myself, a woman is sitting alone doing absolutely nothing. She notices a fly crawling across the table and strikes up a conversation with him. Something terribly dramatic happens, and the poem ends. This happens day after day, as many days as there are poems in a book, leaving her exhausted.

White sadness is the sadness of teeth, bones, fingernails, and stars, yes, but it is also the sadness of cereal, shower caps, and literary foam, it is the sadness of Aunt Jenny's white hair covering her body like a sheet, down to her toes, as she lay on the sickbed, terrifying the children who were brought in one by one to say goodbye. It is the sadness of radio waves traveling through space forever, it is the voice of John Lennon being interviewed, his voice growing weaker and weaker as the waves pass eternally through a succession of galaxies, not quite there, but still...

Brown sadness is the simple sadness. It is the sadness of huge, upright stones. That is all. It is simple. Huge, upright stones surround the other sadnesses, and protect them. A circle of huge, upright stones—who would have thought it?

THEY WERE WRONG

They say a picture is worth a thousand words, but I never believed them. They say all writing is an argument with the world, but I've never met them, and besides, I no longer live in this or any other world. Where do I live? you ask. I live in a fog, a haze, and the drowsy fumes of daylight make me want to sleep. To sleep, you will recall, is to leave this world, and as soon as you wake you must jump on a carousel if you want to catch back up. It makes me yawn, it makes me put ketchup on my eggs which makes a bloody mess. Now I'm tired again and this is serious business. I need some flowers. A little trip, no more than twenty minutes, to the grocery store and back, that will do the wake-up trick. A big fresh bouquet of flowers lolling around in a vase on the table and I'll be fine. Sometimes just looking at something can produce a powerful shock of adrenaline. But you mustn't go further than that—you mustn't bend down to smell the flowers, that would be disastrous, their fumes would bring too much peace: so much peace coursing through your body would cause another yawn. Now I am in my car, I am on my way to the flowers, and I find traffic peaceful when it is backed up at a stoplight. Just sitting here—I'm in the driver's seat of course—with a car in front of me and a car behind me, is profoundly *nice*. It feels right, it feels like everything is exactly the way it is supposed to be, as if everything that ever happened from the beginning of all events, time chief among them, has led to this very line of cars at this very red light; the death of dinosaurs, men and women living in caves, the weaving of cloaks, the whole Middle Ages, the cultivation of maize, the suckling of a little boy who will grow up and die in the wrestling ring—all these things led to this moment, a moment of bluish exhaust rising from the tailpipes of cars as peacefully as smoke from the pipe of an old sailor. Now the light has changed and this historical moment of peace is gone, we are moving forward, I am moving forward towards my flowers and another is moving forward towards his can of soup, still another moving towards, who knows, a sooner death than any of the other customers. In the parking lot I want to sleep but open the door in a great effort to meet the air. Soon I am in the mart itself, I am in the ninth aisle, I am not pushing a cart or anything else, I have never had a baby, I am free and virginal, walking down the aisle on my own two dangling legs, and at the end of the aisle is a garden of leaves and blossoms, I am in the garden, there are plants and flowers, everything is green and alive and growing and there are masses of color to choose from, red, yellow, orange, white, purple, a man is buying flowers for his wife, pink roses wrapped in cellophane—could anything be more idyllic, less argumentative, than that? Yet I want to speak. *Stop*, I say, as the man bends down over his flowers, flowers that will in time move on and belong to his wife, *please don't smell the roses*—but it is too late, he has done it—and now I can smell them, too—the air is saturated with sacred attar—and I, who was so close to being energized, who came all this way from the beginning of time, want nothing now but to fall asleep, to lie down on the floor at the end of the ninth aisle, among the houseplants, and sleep the sleep of ages, having spoken to a man who ignored my sage advice, and now looks as tired of the world as I am.

THE GIFT

The day the living room flooded I had not left the apartment in five days, everything was spotlessly clean, I had no work to do except writing my thoughts in a journal, the thought of which filled me with terror and boredom. That fateful and final morning I was in bed reading, unable to concentrate because of what I had done the day before. The day before I had ordered by telephone a large gift box of glacé apricots from Australia. The catalog, *South Sea Gifts*, showed the fruit in a handsome wooden crate, lined with gold foil. They cost $86.20 and I had them sent to myself with a gift card that said *from Mary to Mary*. I was uneasy because I now had no money to buy groceries with and it would be some time before the apricots arrived, even though I had them sent express, which cost more. I looked forward to their arrival but at the same time they would, when they arrived, only remind me of my stupidity and terrible guilt. My guilt was tremendous. To have used the last of my money sending myself a gift of glacé apricots! And the gold foil—that had cost more, too. The cheaper "home boxes" had more apricots in them, but were without gold foil. The gold foil looked so nice, shining beside the golden apricots. Of course I had been looking at a photograph, and I worried that the picture was somehow "touched up," because I once met a food stylist whose job it was to make photographs of food look better than the food itself; she used glycerin and starch and hairspray to make things luscious and shining, crisp, fresh, mouthwatering in a tantalizing way. I didn't want to open the box and be disappointed. I also thought of ordering a circle of white cotton mosquito netting, but came to my senses. At least I could eat the apricots. What would I do with mosquito netting? I just like the way it looks—you can drape it over anything and the draped thing becomes soft and mysterious. I read an article once about a woman who was an intensely intellectual Buddhist and she wanted to make her house as empty and white as possible, but she owned thousands of books, which dragged the energy of the space down, so she simply made vertical pillars of her books and draped them with mosquito netting and got the effect she was after—the effect of owning nothing, wanting nothing, living in a windswept environment of peace. All my extravagant mail-ordering—it had me feeling uneasy. I felt vapid and shallow and guilty, I loved my books and just the sight of them strewn around on low-lying tables and lined up on windowsills and stacked on the floor—along with catalogs and unopened bills—had always made me feel happy in a teeming, chaotic way, and gave me the feeling my life was full and interesting, that I was a serious and charming person. I also worried about the people who answered the phone for the catalog companies—did they have enough to eat? Did they ever steal a glacé apricot or two? I knew they had work, they had to answer phone calls, they had to calm the caller down and answer all her questions, they had to explain the difference between a "gift box" and a "home box." I could see them in a cavernous room, sitting in makeshift booths with earphones on. For some reason I draped them all with mosquito netting, I mean each one individually wore a cocoon of soft white gauze. It muffled their voices while they spoke to the customer, she had to ask them to repeat what they just said, so an endless loop of repetition began to bubble up from the cocoons. That's how I pictured it. It was then that I heard the water in the living room, bubbling up from some mysterious source. I got out of bed to investigate and as soon as I entered the hall I saw a pool of brown water advancing toward my feet. I had forgotten to put on slippers, I was standing in my bare feet, and the brown water came up over my ankles. I waded forward toward the living room. The sofa was covered with mud and pieces of debris—sticks and clumps of leaves, the black gunk that closes off a rain gutter. There was a high-water mark on the television screen, a wavy white salt horizon that crossed the black glass. My books, too, were covered with the wavy lines of loose, disintegrating matter—detritus, I believe it is called. Some piglets were scavenging the place, eating the stuffing out of a chair in the corner, a chair I always read in. Why did I decide to read in bed that morning? I don't know. It was highly unusual. Everything was waterlogged, the legs of the table looked soft, like they were made of oatmeal, and a mass riot of spiders swarmed on top of my table, the way I've seen ants swarm under my welcome mat outside. The flood had obviously subsided. It must have happened during the night when I was sleeping. I thought for a moment that there was a bloated corpse on the floor, but it was just a sack of rotten potatoes that had floated out from under the sink and was stranded in the stagnant water, a gelatinous mass, puffed up and green. I'm ashamed to say my first thought was that I could not possibly clean up this mess by myself; I needed help. And what about those piglets in the corner, devouring my chair? Where did they come from? The place stank. It smelled worse than a sewer. It smelled like a petri dish of primordial ooze and whoever I called for help would have to cordon off more than my living room: the entire building and the block it sat upon would have to be cordoned off too. And in this way another day of potential reverie had been broken in two, utterly destroyed by my desire for an apricot, a single indiscretion for which my habitat had become a village of sticks on the banks of a rising river, where trade winds blew and the rains came and mosquitoes bred; and where mosquitoes breed, one will be needing some netting.

THE INVASIVE THING

In the beginning I suppose there were crumbs, a little something that fell from the crack of the mouth, a chip off the hunk. These crumbs on my kitchen counter look like a scattering of stars, though they are not much bigger than grains of salt, and made of toast, burnt bread. There are those (I have seen them too) who do not notice such things as crumbs, and if pointed out to them, consider crumbs as natural as a tree and as unremarkable as anything that goes unnoticed. But a tree! A tree is a gigantic plant, the most gigantic plant on the planet. Nothing is larger than a tree, unless it is man-made or made of rock. In this trees are remarkable, beyond any individual characteristics each may possess (I once saw a picture of a cactus with cancer which was beautiful in its branching mutations). Most things, I have noticed, have the right to exist and stay as they are. My hand, for example, has a mind of its own. I cannot say who sees the crumbs first, my eyes or my hands, but my fingers begin to crouch in preparation for what happens next: I move the crumbs with my crouching hand over the edge of the counter, where they fall into the palm of my other hand, which began to open as soon as the other began to crouch. I do not know which is the Invasive Thing, my hands or the crumbs, for the invasive plant grows wild and free, cancer cells multiply with joy and a mind of their own, and the planets inhabit what was once an infinite emptiness we do our own small part in filling, not only by existing (even if unnoticed) but also by all our minute and repetitive actions, such as cleaning crumbs from a countertop, which is as empty now as it ever was, and the crumbs sealed in the total darkness of a black plastic bag that sooner or later I will carry out.

THE SUBLIME

Had no warning of what to expect, no sign of sharp curves. Hadn't gone far when I came to hairpin turns every few hundred feet—on both sides of me deep canyons with only a few scrimpy bushes between me and the Abyss. My hair stood on end. The road was narrow then narrower, turning this way and that as I climbed, hunched over the steering wheel. Could see from the corner of my eye that there was an incredible view, but couldn't look.

A STRANGE THING

Maybe I read this, or dreamt it, for my mind wanders as I age, but I have always believed Odysseus, when he heard the sirens, was hearing *The Odyssey* being sung, and in fear of being seduced by his own story he had himself bound. And he was in even greater fear of hearing the end, for he could not bear the possibility he might become someone other than who he was now, a war hero of great courage and unexcelled strategy, trembling against the cords at his own mast. Or he might become an even greater man, one without a single fear in the world, one who would balk at a man having to tie himself up in fear of anything, and then it would be revealed that the man he was now was actually a coward. Either way, he felt doomed as he sailed past his own story. He sailed past the island, he sailed past the sirens just as they were coming to the end, and once out of earshot he did a strange thing, of which there is no record, the story having ended in some faraway sound that was no more distinguishable than an eyedropper of sweetness in the vast and salty sea.

THE BOOK

Dear friends, this is for you

"They're gone now. It makes me sad to think about it.
Feeling old, for no reason at all
I picked a bit of mint from the ditch."
— Francis Jammes

UNTITLED

About this time I began to suspect I was never named; people called me Mary because it was convenient, or because they had heard others call me Mary, I was in the beginning named after someone else who was named Mary but I was neither this person nor the one they called Mary after her, I was nameless, and in this state I perpetually wandered among fruit and flowers and foliage, among vines and overhanging rock and untamed animals, none of whom I could name, none of whom knew my name, nor, if they did, could they speak it. I read once that the Amazon was called the Green Hell, and if that is a name, I take it, if only as a substitute for my unknown name, which not even my parents knew when they named me Mary, after a woman who scrubbed her kitchen floor on her hands and knees, once a week, with a stiff brush. She was kind to me and I loved her, and since her death I have dreamt of her many times, either searching for her or speaking to her, but never once in my dreams have I called her Mary, which, I suspect, is not her name, or if it once was, is no longer.

THE PHOTOGRAPH

I have a photograph that was taken more than a hundred years ago. I am related to its subject but don't know who she is, I don't know whether I am related to her through my mother or through my father, they hadn't been born when the photograph was taken and they are dead now. I don't know where the picture was taken except on the porch steps of an old wooden house, and I stare at her who is sitting on the steps, about thirty with dark hair, looking like no one I know, almost expressionless before the camera, I stare at her and it *looks* like she is looking at me but I know she hasn't a clue that she is looking at me, she looks right through me, she is looking at her photographer, and I think I see a strand of hair about to fall over one eye, maybe she is thinking about that, I don't know, but there is a deep and abiding bond between us, I feel it, even if she doesn't know my mother's name or my father's name, whether they lived past infancy or at all. We are both alive, she in the picture and I with the picture in my hands, and we both know nothing of the other—perhaps that is the bond between us, though she is certainly not thinking about the future in which *I* am the unknown relative. And then I realize she *is* thinking about the future, she is *waiting* for the future, she is waiting for the small unmistakable sound of the shutter, the click of the camera signifying that something is over, and I do not think we can be any more specific than that, so I blink and let that be the sign between us.

PIXIE

It was the day of my first haircut, which was the day of my last haircut, it was the day of my first trip to the hairdresser, which was the day of my last, it was what I might now call the Day of the Great Shorning, for I was led like a lamb by my mother through the door of the glass-fronted shop, the door had curly black lettering painted right on the glass (I couldn't read, I was wearing a dress) and then we were in a room full of women, I called them ladies then, they were all talking at once (how did they find so many things to do with their mouths?) but my mother was not talking, she was whispering the way she whispered on Christmas Eve or the morning of my birthday, and I felt a great surprise was in store for me, or so it seemed when I was caped like a princess and set on a throne, a big padded chair, the chair itself was a surprise for it turned like a planet, and as if it were night I was turned away from the light, I was no longer facing the mirror, and though my back was to the light there were wonderful things to look at, potions were lined up on shelves, bottles full of colored water, one had a comb suspended in it like a shark in the aquarium, perhaps I would be able to take it home, it would look nice in my room, I was so intent on taking it home (I would have to buy fish food) I didn't hear the scissors, I didn't hear my own hair falling from off my head and onto the floor, but when I looked down I could see the lifeless piles of it scattered like chicken feed (would I be sent to a farm?) and then the planet spun round again and I was looking in the mirror at the face of a stranger, a hairless pixie with the ears of an elf, and she so scared me (I had heard you could be frightened to *death*) I leapt out of my throne like a dolphin (my aunt and uncle lived near the ocean, I could go to them) and ran through the door with the curly black lettering (it looked like seaweed to me now), I was through the door and down the street when I collided with my mother, it was brutal, but even in those moments my hair was starting to grow back (*it would grow back in time* was what my mother said, and so it did), it grew through the years until I could toss it, now it is like a bridal train when I walk, it wraps me like an octopus when I bathe, but the child who wanted to feed a comb is unrecognizable to me, and belongs to another century.

THE WRAPPED BOOK

A long, long time ago I lived briefly in Switzerland, in an Alpine village with a single bookstore, one which sold books in many languages, including English, and whenever they sold a book they would wrap it in plain blue paper and tie it with string, like a present. I had never seen such a custom and loved it. I decided to always keep a book wrapped in plain blue paper on my shelves, some book I knew I would love, some book whose title and author I would have forgotten by the time I unwrapped it. And so I did, for years, but more often than not by the time I unwrapped the book it was a book I had already read, or a book that I did not exactly love. Still, it was of great solace to me to have a wrapped book on my shelves. I have such a book now and am afraid to open it, it is not in plain blue paper but in shiny paper, a shiny photograph of some rocky island in some blue sea. A magazine page? It has sat among my books for many years, how many I cannot say. I have no idea what book is inside. I will open it one day but not today. I want to be surprised, I want the book to delight me, I want it to be the most perfect book in the world, but I am afraid of being disappointed. I know when I wrapped the book it seemed perfect to me, but times have changed and I have changed and all my hopes have been redirected. It seems I believe in a bygone world though I no longer live there. Will I continue to read about all that is dusty? I am not brave enough to open the book wrapped in an island in the middle of a sea I cannot name. *Strait Is the Gate* is the name of the book I bought in the Alpine village, and took home and ripped open.

NETTLES

If everyone were a storyteller, the infrastructure of the village would collapse. With more than one teller—with so many—contention and conflict would ensue. The one true storyteller—who can say which one?—would be compelled to retire to a cave and sit silent for ten years, eating nothing but nettles and drinking the tea that can be made from them. When he (she? they?) came out, the village would be going about its daily business, digging tubers, nursing babies, drying meat, all of which had already been put into a story by everyone else, so that no story would be left to tell, except the story of the one true storyteller, how he had lived in a cave for ten years, nettled by his own silence, and had at last emerged and found no one willing to listen.

THE BARK

I took my dog to the lake, he stood at the water's edge and barked, the echo of his bark came back and he barked at it, again and again he barked at his own echo, thinking there was another dog on the other side of the lake. *Welcome to poetry*, I said.

NOPE

I was in a big city and visited its famous independent bookstore. It was huge, I had trouble finding the poetry and had to ask for help. I sat myself down on the floor in front of all the poetry and looked over the titles. There were so many! I found poets I loved, poets who were my friends, poets I had known who were now dead, poets I had met once and never seen again (but always remembered), poets I had never heard of, all manner of poets, but all these books just made me sad in the end—I knew nobody read them. *I* read them, but when I did I just started writing poems myself, creating an endless loop that depressed me. Just then a teenaged boy passed by with his mother, they paused in front of the poetry section and the boy said "Look! I found the poetry, Dad is always telling me to look for the poetry, to find the poetry—well, here it is, I've found it!" He was making a joke at his father's expense, but his mother seemed moved, for she said "Would you like to buy a book of poetry?" and the boy said "Nope!" and ambled away. A wave of ridiculous but deep happiness swept over me, suddenly I was feeling so happy I got up and left the store without buying a single book.

WE NEED TO TALK ABOUT ICE CREAM

Choose five artists you deeply admire for being extraordinary and make a documentary film in which each one is shown, for ten minutes, in violent argument with their spouse or partner, revealing the artist's mean, low, reprehensible side.

THE CANDY

I was not even sure I wanted to see him once more before he died, and if I did it seemed a kind of madness, he meant nothing to me now, less than nothing, but the cold mountainous landscape in which we met, and in which I knew he still lived, had haunted me for half of a century. When I lie sleepless at night, I count snowflakes the way some people count sheep, I have a friend who counts sheep and she told me the sheep are really little lambs jumping over a low wooden fence, but this, I think, is no different than counting horses or dogs. The snow I see falls, it cannot be mistaken for anything other than large flat white crystals, no two alike, and I count them horizontally, on a plane of sorts, for they are falling side by side through the air, slowly and continuously, accumulating on the ground. We, he and I, walked through such snow on the evening we met, and when we reached my door (he was walking me home after an evening spent in the company of a great many others) we began to retrace our steps through the snow, walking back to the place we had started from, we did this without a word between us, it was an unspoken agreement that we did not want the walk to come to an end and therefore repeated it, I cannot say how many repetitions we made of our walk, but a ten-minute walk lasted more than an hour. Neither of us spoke as we walked, not a word passed between us, but one can listen to falling snow, anyone who does not believe this has never walked silently through the veil of it, if rain can speak why not snow, the way a wet, sobbing heart can still be heard beating when it is cold and withdrawn. It snowed for five days. The house I lived in was buried in snow and time became fainter and fainter until neither of us knew what day it was and had to ask the other *what day is it? is it Friday or Saturday? was it Sunday or Monday?* We could not remember and we always disagreed, about that and a great many other things, as it happened. It was cold, it was messy, I didn't like it (later I moved to the desert), once my parents had taken me as a girl to the German Alps, it was a skiing holiday, and while my parents skied, for they were athletic and to their great disappointment I was not, I joined a bus tour with the elderly (elderly to me then, I am of their age now), we crossed into Austria to visit the famous castle of mad King Ludwig (we were told the Disneyland castle was based on its very pinnacles) but the castle bored me, all I remember is that when the king disagreed with a dinner guest, he opened a trapdoor beneath the table and his guest fell a long way into a cold stone dungeon; that was one day, it snowed that day and all of the other days, days I spent sitting in our rented chalet reading a novel while eating chocolates from a box, I picked one up and ate it without even bothering to look at it, each piece was nestled in an indentation, the indentations were on a single sheet of molded brown plastic, and when the chocolates were gone I turned the molding upside down and it looked like the little village of houses we were staying in—I did like the snow on the roofs of the houses, and the snow on the mountaintop was magnificent, even if the skiers were repeatedly streaking down it in a kind of madness, like tears, or what struck me as tears when seen from below, or above, or standing a little ways off to the side, I mean the madness, the past, the fantasy, the trapdoor, whatever leads to the future.

HOUSE HUNTING

When we lived in the blue house we were happy. But it didn't have a porch or a fireplace, and we knew these things would make us happier. That was when we bought the yellow house with a porch and a fireplace, and we were happy in the summer sitting on our porch, and happy in the winter sitting in front of the fire, but we weren't happy in the kitchen or the bedroom or the living room of that yellow house, fall and spring were especially hard, when it was too cold to use the porch and too warm to build a fire. That was when we bought the white house, where we were happy in the kitchen and in the bedroom and in the living room, and we had a porch and a fireplace—having once had them we would never give them up. The porch was smaller than our first porch but we didn't mind a bit. The fireplace was larger, though, and even if the fire was roaring all the heat in the house went straight up the chimney and we began to actually shiver. We were so cold we put on our coats and went for a drive, we drove past the blue house and looked at it with nostalgia, we drove past the yellow house and got a lump in our throats, but not so big we couldn't swallow it. On our way home we passed a red house with no one in it, there was no For Sale sign but we decided to have a look anyway, we walked around the red house and peeked in all the windows, and there were a great many of them. So much light and privacy! The house was set back from the road and had an enormous yard behind it, it seemed to go on forever and then continue into the woods that bordered on a state park that bordered on a national one. With so much privacy we wouldn't need a porch, and with so much light we wouldn't need a fire. But without a For Sale sign, who should we call? We decided to ask around, so we drove to the nearest house and knocked on the door. Is the house next door for sale? we asked. The red house? they said. It's been like that for years. But who lives there? we said. No one, they said, but the deer like it so much they come at every dusk to graze. Who owns it? we asked. Why, we do, they said, it's ours to look at, we bought it so we could see the deer, we can sit out in the evenings and watch them grazing. Will you sell it? we asked. If we lived there you could still see the deer. I doubt it, they said. The deer like their privacy, they aren't happy when people are around. We pleaded, but those crummy happy people wouldn't budge. So we said goodbye to the happy deer, who, it turns out, were an endangered breed of tiny reindeer with spots and delicate antlers.

A LESSON IN HISTORY

My student hated history. History is stupid, he said. Stuff that's already happened is boring. Maybe a history of parties might be slightly interesting, like on one page or something, but there's no history of parties because you go to a party to forget history—that's the point. You party. Only an idiot doesn't get it. If you remember anything, it wasn't a party. Jesus. Ok, take him. The only thing you need to know about Jesus is that he's famous for throwing a dinner party. Take the Greek tragedies. The famous plays and stuff. People who have read them are so proud of it, but wasn't it pride that did old man Eddie in? What a pussy. Cultured people are so blind they can't see what makes them civilized: it's pride. It's insane. They might as well eat powdered glass. We do that at parties sometimes.

MY LIFE AS A SCHOLAR

My friend the metalsmith told me that the first piece of jewelry she learned to make as an apprentice was a fibula, the earliest form of a pin, used by the ancient Greeks and Romans to fasten their togas. It is used today on Scottish kilts, in miniature we call it a safety pin, and until the advent of disposable diapers it was the ubiquitous diaper pin. I was teaching undergraduates at the time, and immediately signed up to teach the Greek tragedies—Oedipus, upon learning that he had gone to bed with his mother, stabbed out his eyes with a diaper pin!

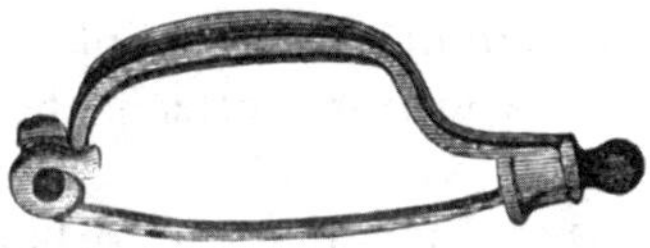

THE CASHEW

Throughout the play, a man or woman is sleeping on a divan set to the side of the stage (where it will not interfere with the comings and goings of the actors). Ideally, the sleeper is curled in the shape of a cashew. At no particular moment, but once during each act, the sleeper half-rises and, as if from a window of lucidity, says, "I'm trying to stay calm." This "character," whoever he is (a stranger thrust into the circumstances unfolding around him? the playwright? Shakespeare? Brecht?) then resumes his peaceful sleep.

These stage directions may be introduced into any play, but if they are introduced into all plays, is it certain or doubtful that the course of theater has been changed?

Keep your essay to a minimum of five hundred words.

MY MEMORY OF A STORY BY LYDIA DAVIS I READ YEARS AGO AND *NEVER FORGOT*

A Russian, Wassilly, is mysteriously escorted to a snowbound village in the Eastern wilds. On the way there, bells ring in the icy air. A sleigh? In the village, which is practically empty, strangers act in strange and unsettling ways. Dogs begin to bark. Faces peer out of the windows. Dogs continue to bark. As the story ends, the thin cold air is filled with faint and faraway barks...

THE STAGEHAND

My job is to remove the shoes from the stage floor at the end of the first act, those belonging to the Countess, sweet low-heeled slippers of rose-colored satin with a square marcasite buckle. And again at the end of the third act, only this time there are three pairs, those of the dead Countess and her lover, and those of the witless Count who has murdered them before killing himself. I remove the shoes at the end so none of the actors will trip over them when they take their curtain call, which is when I stand in the wings and think *if it weren't for me there would be a disaster.*

THE TREES

It will soon be noon. You may put on your hat, and we will go out. It is a hot day, so we will sit in the cool shade of the trees. We can see the flowers in bloom and hear the birds sing. When it is cool we will go back to the house. We have cut down those trees that were near, for they made a dark shade, and there was a deep gloom in my room.

WHAT HAPPENS WHEN YOU DIE

As it happens, I travel a lot, therefore I am in a good position to know what happens when you die. When you die, a plane takes off, another plane lands, people of all ages travel rapidly forward on the moving sidewalk between terminals. A traveler between connections stops at a kiosk and buys a damp turkey sandwich, another one buys a fruit smoothie and still another, weary but with more time, stops for a beer at the airport bar. A man in the gift shop buys a box of molasses candy for his wife, while a woman he thinks attractive picks up a plastic airplane for her son. A flight attendant rolls her bag effortlessly through security. An airline employee at gate 32 deals with an irate passenger, who will afterwards feel guilty for ruining her day. There is a small crisis in the bathroom, swiftly attended to. The electric cart moving between gates carries a passenger who can no longer walk, and barely misses running into one who can. A plane is late. Another one is early. All this happens when you die, and if you don't believe me you are alone, and stranded beyond help.

THE CLOUD BEATERS

It was a winter's noon, ice-cold and sunny, when I saw in a single bare tree a hundred or more birds flitting in and out of the branches, lunching on withered berries. The sun hit the breasts of the birds and they all shone like hammered gold. I described this event to my friend and she asked what kind of birds they were. But I could not remember the name of the birds, the word had receded to a space in my mind I could not reach. "Cloud Beaters" came out of my mouth—where that came from I'll never know, it may be it came from the same place the forgotten word lived. "Oh, cedar waxwings!" she cried. I had struggled, I had tried, I had come as close as I could, I didn't have the words, but she knew what I meant.

THE TRANSLATOR

Two insects exchanged information in the middle of the night. Perhaps they were frogs, I can't say, but the shrilling carried far; I woke in my bed and did not turn on the light, four times the information was relayed and came back verbatim, or maybe countered with questions, *did I hear you correctly? are you absolutely certain? could you repeat it?* And then they quit. A phone call after midnight means accident or death (I have received both) and though I know it may have been a creaturely announcement of love and ripeness (those too) it sounded like dire info to my ear. I lay there, wondering. Was it something that I, too, would like to know or needed unbeknownst to know, something that would affect me personally, if only I knew? What *were* they saying, out there in the night? To pay such close attention, to hear with every fiber of my being, and remain completely ignorant.

GOLDEN CRUMBS

Ever, when the two ladies were having a quiet cup of tea in the great, big, uncomfortable drawing-room on the first floor, with its conventional wilderness of chairs and silly little tables laden with uninteresting bric-a-brac, they heard the front doorbell ring, and began to speculate who the visitor might be. Week after week, on a Tuesday a little after four, the bell rang once and once only, there was silence thereafter, and as the years passed the two ladies came to regard this event as the great mystery of their lives.

LOVE STORY

The one winter I spent by water I would walk out on the ice every evening at dusk after the ice fishermen had abandoned their shanty. I would peer into the window of stapled plastic and watch the stick of frozen butter as it lay there on a plywood counter. I don't know what the butter was for. I knew they built fires on the ice for warmth and drank out of bottles for warmth, but butter in the shanty? I never saw them actually cook, they would take the fish home, home not being the shanty, the shanty being a temporary winter dwelling where they could store their gear and stuff. The sun would set, throwing a glare on the ice, and sometimes I saw through the window that it cast a glare on that stick of butter. I went back every day to check on the butter. It was never unwrapped, it was never cut. And then spring came, overnight the shanty sank on a doily of slush and the butter went with it. I never asked, I never found out, but as the days grew warmer, warm enough to melt butter over an afternoon, I often thought to myself that it was the perfect love story, and I was glad the butter had disappeared overnight and not stuck around to melt.

THE WIND

I once received a two-page letter—typed, single-spaced—with nothing in it. The individual words had meaning, as all words do, but when you set the meanings side by side they became meaningless. I must have read that letter three or four times before I realized the only thing I actually knew was that I felt empty and sad and the world felt drained of beauty on account of that letter with nothing in it. As I ripped the letter up—I had been reading it at a picnic table—a sudden gust of wind blew the many fragments of paper into a nearby bush. It was suddenly very interesting—the bush not the letter—so I photographed it, then forgot about it. Weeks later I had the film developed and there was the letter in many pieces, each of which had snagged somewhere on the bush. I could still read some of the words. And that photo had meaning, looking at it I saw at once it had meaning, while the letter had had none. I think this has something to do with art.

THE COLOR

I was at my desk pretending to be writing. Actually I *really was* writing, but while writing I was really thinking about things that had nothing to do with what I was writing—and there were quite a few of them—and even now I must stop and think about that strange phrase *quite a few*, for how can there be *quite a few*, if there are few there are few, but wouldn't *quite a few* be a lot, quite a lot as a matter of fact? Now I am done thinking about that, but this morning, while pretending to write, I was thinking that I had made a terrible mistake in choosing the fabric of my new curtains, no, not the fabric but the *color* of the fabric (to be exact) (and one must strive for something), the color was too light, it needed to be ten shades darker, not a light wheat-colored straw but a dark golden straw, clearly I had made a terrible mistake and was now deeply in debt to my better judgment, such as it is (there are days my better judgment and I are not even on speaking terms), and there I sat, on and on I sat, pretending to write but secretly obsessed with what I had done, what I had done of my own free will, such as it is. I had irreversibly chosen, out of all the colors in the world, *the wrong one*. A titanic mistake! And as I sat there, many past instances of identical horror came back to me, like ghosts who were hungry and came home to eat everything they could lay their hands on, which was quite a lot. How could I pretend to be writing when the room was full of ghosts, when all my mistakes were hovering over me, demanding my attention, gobbling, always gobbling something? I could pretend to pretend—the thought occurred to me—it had worked in the past—but the ghosts wouldn't fall for it, I knew that, they would be thinking *there she is, pretending to be writing, her old ploy, what a scam.* And so I tricked them, I no longer pretended to be writing, I just stopped, I stopped suddenly and cleanly, throwing them a loop I hoped would take them out the window.

THE PERK

He was just a clown. Of medium height, a little fat, a little clumsy. I don't remember his name but I remember the day I called the pizza parlor and asked if they could arrange a child's birthday party for my husband, who was turning fifty. My husband was boyish, had a terrific sense of humor and loved pizza, so my bright idea was a child's party with balloons and paper hats and a clown. Plus each guest got to go into the kitchen and make their own pizza. They did all that stuff for children. The manager of the pizza parlor told me it wasn't possible, they wouldn't do it for an adult, it was too weird. I was so disappointed I asked if I might leave my name and number in case he changed his mind. Think it over, I said. I don't think he wanted to think it over, but not wanting to be impolite he agreed to take my name and number. When I gave him my name there was a pause before he said Mary Ruefle, the poet? I was completely taken aback, as far as I knew I wasn't known to anyone, except maybe four people in another state. That's me, I said. The manager explained that he had an MFA, he had read my work and enjoyed it, and he'd be happy to let me throw a kid's party for my husband in his pizza parlor. Again I was taken aback, because there were no known perks to being a poet, and here was a pizza joint rolling out the red carpet. So I threw my husband the party. I thought our clown would be wearing a ruffled, polka-dotted jumpsuit but he was in a plain shirt and tie with a plastic clown mask over his face. He did a few magic tricks and twisted long balloons into dachshunds–I remember that because it seemed to me an amazing skill. One of the things the clown always did was to read a fairy tale to the kids, and for us he chose Hans Christian Andersen's "The Little Match Girl," where a poor little barefoot girl is wandering the streets on a bitterly cold and snowy night, trying to sell matches. If she goes home her father will beat her, for she hadn't sold a single match. To warm herself she strikes one match after another, and has a series of beautiful fantasies. In the morning she's found dead, frozen to death on the street. It was very strange, no one knew what to say, but we managed to have fun when we were in the kitchen making our own pizzas, and laughed about "The Little Match Girl" while throwing disks of pepperoni in the air, pretending they were matches. A few weeks later my husband, who was also a doctor, was called to the fourth floor of the hospital, the psych ward. As he walked down the hall to see a patient who had some object stuck up his nose, he saw the clown in a hospital gown shuffling towards him. Hello birthday boy, the clown said, and feebly waved. My husband asked him what he was doing there, on the psych ward; the clown said he had lost his job as a clown and had tried to kill himself. I am very sorry, my husband said, you were such a good clown. My husband came home that night and relayed the conversation. Neither of us could quite believe it, it was so sad. We lived out in the country on a dirt road and our closest neighbor, whom we didn't know, was six acres away. One day I walked past our neighbor's house and there was a trailer next to the house, a trailer with an open end facing the road. There was the clown, sitting at a little table inside, with a cot beside the table and something tacked on the wall. He looked up and saw me, our eyes met, and his face seemed to me to light up, just a glimmer, and then he waved at me, a feeble wave but still a wave. For a couple of days we waved at each other whenever I walked by, and one day the trailer was gone and I never saw him again, so

I don't know how the story ends. Or where he is, or even if he's living. But we did return to the pizza parlor—the manager always came personally to "the poet's table"—and we asked why the clown had lost his job, and were told parents complained that all his stories were grim, and terrorized the children. And then we ordered a 16″ white pizza with spinach, artichokes, and garlic.

THE HEART, WHAT IS IT?

I was tired of writing my name and address on the corner of envelopes so I decided to have an inkstamp made. Standing in the store I realized that such stamps accommodate three lines. Three lines! That was the number of lines in a common haiku, so I immediately decided to have a haiku stamp made instead. But standing there I could not remember a single haiku by my favorite haiku master, Issa, so I gave them one I could remember, by Ikkyū, a fifteenth-century Zen monk and poet who was born and died in Kyōto.

> The heart, what is it,
> is it the sound of the pinetrees
> blowing in the painting?

When I went back to pick up the completed stamp, I was overcome with the feeling I had gotten it wrong, that I had misremembered the haiku; I could not shake this feeling so I called my friend Elena, a poet and translator, who had first introduced me to this haiku, which was her favorite. She said I had indeed gotten it wrong, Ikkyū's haiku was

> The heart, what is it,
> is it the sound of the pinetrees
> there in the painting?

I told her about the stamp and the word *blowing*, which suddenly I liked; she said that *there* was better because it left so much more to the imagination of the reader.

My argument in favor of *blowing* was that it didn't make much of a difference since the central—most important—words in the haiku came at the end—*in the painting*. Those words blew everything out of the water, they contradicted the idea of any sound whatsoever. The poem's power came from those three last words.

I called my friend Jody, a poet and translator, and asked her which version she preferred. She said *blowing* because it was more specific and an active verb. When someone agrees with you, it feels very good.

Then I asked Michael, my husband and a poet, and he did not hesitate to say he preferred *there*, because *there* suggested that the trees had a more dimensional life, that *blowing* was "too typical for trees."

Then I asked Jody to ask David, her husband, a poet and translator and Zen practitioner, to break the tie by saying which version he preferred. David said he didn't like either version because he didn't like the haiku to begin with—it was full of too many words and "not enough emptiness."

My opinion was that if someone wanted fewer and fewer words and more and more emptiness they shouldn't bother with poetry at all, they should neither read it nor write it but simply live their lives, walking through the city or the forest without a thought to language. I knew in my heart that the outer world was without written language and that pages of writing were ultimately meaningless, I knew all that, but I also knew that humans are peculiar and often lead long lives and try to do things that make them happy, and that writing was one of those ten thousand things.

Then Jody called me back and said she changed her mind, she definitely preferred the version with *there* in it, but that she would change the punctuation to

> The heart, what is it,
> is it the sound of the pinetrees
> there—in the painting?

But I still preferred *blowing* to *there*—I could see the trees bending in the wind and then WHAM I saw the painting, without movement, without sound, and thus was left at a standstill. After heart-movement heart-stillness, that seemed accurate to me. None of us knew Japanese, and I have no idea how many different English translations have been made of the original, but I think Ikkyū could care less about the fate of his poem.

So there it is: Elena, Jody, and Michael prefer *there*, David doesn't like the haiku to begin with, and Ikkyū has no opinion.

I like *blowing* and I will not bend.

As usual, I have given you a piece of my heart.

I DREAM OF JUNG

A friend who was studying Buddhism made a pilgrimage to Tibet. She brought back a gift for me, two oblong pieces of metal, each slightly larger than a postage stamp, and told me she had bought them at a bazaar of sorts, old things sold on the street. They were a bright gold color, though I think made of copper or more probably an odd admixture of metals. Each one was embossed with what looked like flying scarves or banners and a round drum-like object that might have been a prayer wheel. Another friend of mine is a metalsmith, a jeweler, and I had her convert the two pieces into a pair of dangling earrings. Sometime later I had the dream: I was invited to Carl Jung's house for dinner, it was a party of around twelve people, and I wore the earrings; several of the guests admired them, and Jung himself came over to take a look. When he saw them he was aghast, horrified, furious, and he began to shout at me, saying it was sacrilege to turn such sacred objects into jewelry, into decorative trinkets. He was so upset he asked me to leave, and I was so deeply ashamed I did leave, but first I used Jung's bathroom and while raising the lid of his toilet I noticed it had been made out of an ancient African mask or shield—he had converted an oval totem into a lid for his john! Now it was my turn to be furious—I was furious at his hypocrisy, but also relieved and amused; I left Jung's house feeling we were comrades after all—brothers in hypocrisy, twin fools, the King & Queen of Cluelessness.

LUCKY DRAGON

God walked into the Lucky Dragon and, in a tired, half-dead voice, ordered a Shanghai spring roll, wonton soup, steamed dumplings, chicken fried rice, egg foo young, moo shu pork, sweet and sour shrimp, and General Tso's chicken. He loved everything, he ate everything, but the twelve fortune cookies that came after he did not care for, so he folded them carefully into the dough of a dozen unborn children, hoping for the best. While the staff remained watching from the kitchen door, God walked out slowly, absolutely full, unable to fly.

MY DYING FRIEND

I was visiting a dying friend in the hospital and passed by a room full of babies who had not yet been given names. They were all lined up in a row, like science projects. Those with names had won a bracelet and been taken away. But those who remained were quite interesting, judging by the sadness already evident in their features. What do I call thee, little lamb lying here on a bed of cotton? I stopped someone in a uniform who was familiar with them. "Come back tomorrow," she said, "they will all be gone."

DEAR FRIENDS

I have had friends, and have them now, but never once did I believe that in my lifetime the word *friend* would have a new, different, other meaning. I knew language evolved and changed over time, I knew there were new words every year to accommodate its growth and that some words changed meaning; but *love, death, flower, fire*? *Friend*? Then one day I picked up a magazine and read an interview with the COO (chief operating officer) of Facebook, perhaps she still is, I don't know, but she was asked how many friends she had and she said, "Over three thousand. I don't know all of them but I have met them in one shape or form." I would rather be antiquated—I would rather die—than make a statement like that. I *know* my friends, I know the sound of their voices, their speech patterns, their inflections, their hand and body gestures, the wet of their eyes, what makes them laugh, what makes them cry, how their nose was broken and how they became beautiful after that, and mysterious, so mysterious I cannot reconstitute them even as I try, because they are *people*, they walk on this earth, and they will die here.

As Frances Burnett wrote, there are only a few times in life when we think we are going to live forever. And I think one of them is when we are with our friends, laughing, eating, looking each other in the eye. I would rather write about friends than relations. Relations—parents, children, siblings, spouses—exist within a grid of social conceptions and expectations that have evolved over centuries, and though we may fail in these relations, though we may let the preconceived down, nowhere in these relations do I find the sheer unexpected *variety* that friendship offers, for no two friendships are based on the same thing, the bond between two friends has no explanation other than itself.

I have a friend who has never read a single word I have ever written. I love being with her.

I have a friend who is not a person I could ever be, even if I tried, nor would I want to be, and I love being with her.

I had a friend who peeled an orange in public for the first time when she was seventeen. I do not remember the first time I peeled an orange, but it was probably in front of another. Do any of us remember such an act, such a little act lost in so many other acts performed for the first time when we are children? My friend's mother was cultivated to the point of exoticism, and at the same time conservative and strict; at least that is how I remember her. She taught her daughter that to peel an orange, or any other fruit, in the presence of another person was perverse; you might as well undress in front of them. Fruit was peeled in the kitchen by servants and served naked on a plate with a little knife to the side. The logic of this is itself perverse—do not undress in public but appear there naked—and as a result of such logic my friend was apprehensive when I unpacked our lunch one sunny afternoon, spreading a blue napkin on the stone steps of a cathedral; we were two teenagers having an outing in the city, an adventure, and I had thought to bring a picnic. Hence two unpeeled oranges appeared on the napkin and I watched my friend's face change color as she told me the rules regarding oranges. I insisted that people did it all the time, no one would notice, not a head would turn if she ventured to try. Never before or since have I seen someone peel an orange with such exquisite delicacy. She took off the skin as if it were covered with tiny mother-of-pearl buttons, and her hands trembled every time a piece of skin came off and fell away like a little continent set adrift, revealing the flesh inside, which was sometimes translucent and bright and bursting with moisture, and at other times covered by a thin white cottony undergarment. And that was that, we ate our oranges in public as carelessly as any two girls, none of the passersby noticed anything historical, and years later when I ran into my old friend, and recalled that afternoon in the sun, she told me she hated oranges and never ate them, her mother was dead, and she had no memory of any picnic on the steps of a church.

I had a friend who loved apple trees and apple blossoms and apple orchards, he loved swimming in ponds and lakes, and making currant jam and jam from mulberries and playing the harmonica, but when he read, for he loved books, he read heavy German tomes. He was diagnosed with cancer and the treatment for his cancer caused a stroke that led to blindness, he was blind at the end, and I took him swimming in a lake, I held his hand and helped him wade out until the water was waist-high, and then I said that I would be his beacon, I would not move. And he swam, not far, not much, but he went under and came up utterly refreshed, and all the while I stood there with my arms outstretched and thought *look at me, look at me, I am helping a blind man swim*. And when my friend died, I actually felt *lucky* because my last words to him were *I love you*, and his last words to me were *I love you* and I thought that it didn't get any luckier than that, though of course it could have been luckier: he could have lived with his sight for the last few years of his life, he could have seen his apple trees and gone swimming without my help.

I had a friend in high school, I had a crush on him, he was gay but I didn't know it. I had other friends who were gay and my favorite teachers were gay but I didn't know it, and there were other teachers who were not gay and not my favorite who were having sex with students who were not my friends but I didn't know it, I found out years later, my friend told me all about it, and I was shocked. We were in our thirties then, and he was dying of AIDS. I mean, he had AIDS and knew he would probably die but was not certain; he didn't want to die but he did come to see me, twice, in what turned out to be the last year of his life. We sat in a diner in the middle of Michigan and he told me all this stuff that was going on in high school that I had been completely unaware of. None of the gay guys in high school had come out, and he talked about that, about how he knew I had a crush on him but he couldn't bring himself to tell me he was gay. We actually laughed about it, we were in our thirties and considered ourselves grown-ups, adults. Later I found out that I was not grown-up at thirty, but he never found out, he died before he could find out he wasn't a grown-up. Sitting in the diner I said to him *I am so sorry*. And he said *why, because I am gay?* I said *no, not that; because you are going to die*. And he said *I don't want to die, but, you know, these things happen*. These things happen—I think in that moment I must have grown up, but later I lapsed into childhood again, and it was another thirty years before I remembered his words—*these things happen*—and by then I had lost countless friends and family members, by then his words seemed the simplest statement of the truth I had ever heard. After the diner he wanted to take a strenuous hike through the dunes of Lake Michigan, he had had chemo and was weak but was determined to try this one thing while he still had the chance. He barely made it, we would stop every few yards so he could rest, but he would not give up or turn back, and when we reached the shore of the lake he opened his fly and pissed right into the water, I saw his penis for the first time, he had a huge grin on his face and he took off his baseball cap—he was bald beneath it—and waved it in the air like he was riding a bronco in a rodeo. His lover was at the opera when he died, and his mother called me to tell me her son was gone. I had never met her, and she said to me *he talked about you a lot in high school, and at the end—but I never understood—what was the nature of your relationship?* I could tell this was awkward for her, that in her grief she wanted to know everything she could about her son's life and wondered whether he had had sexual relations with women as well as men. I told her the truth, I said *your son was my friend, we were always friends, he was a friend of mine, and I was very lucky.*

I have a friend who believes that birds have souls but humans do not. Although this may sound like the belief of a misanthrope, my friend is anything but that, she is unfaltering in her cheerfulness and kindness, she plays ping-pong and badminton with relish, and though she has suffered the blows and disappointments of life like the rest of us, they have never laid a mantle on her shoulders, and I have often wondered if her explication of souls is connected to her sense of contentment, if it is the secret key to a disposition we could all use. I have known her for most of my life, and she remains a mystery. Birds! Little brown birds!

I had a friend in high school with whom I felt a deep bond; we were both interested in religion and philosophy. In college she went the way of the Greek classics and, by a turn in the road, became a Buddhist. I went the way of English literature and, by a turn in the road, became a poet with a Zen approach to writing who used the word *God* in every third poem. When we were teenagers, we shared the belief that we were human beings on a spiritual journey, but by the time we were fifty we both pretty much knew we were spiritual beings on a human journey, and we expressed this belief by exchanging Christmas cards every December. We didn't see each other in all that time, and then one year I happened to be teaching near her and we managed to spend a day together. We were both divorced and living alone by then, and of course we had lunch in a nifty restaurant (she was a vegetarian, I was not) but the rest of the afternoon we spent in the old swimming pool behind my crumbling apartment complex (the Eden Roc, pink stucco, or what was left of it). And what did we do in the swimming pool? Not swim. We stood waist-deep in the water and saved the lives of hundreds of drowning wasps, picking them one by one out of the water while we lazily talked, without either of us mentioning the wasps and what we were doing for them; for three hours we stood there and had a rhythm going, wasp up wasp out, and I can't remember any of our chat, I only remember the wasps in a pile on the side of the pool, coming to realize in their squirming that they were still alive, though most of them crawled right back into the pool and we saved their lives twice. It was lovely to see my old friend again, but that afternoon we didn't quite act like human friends, we acted like reincarnated lotus buds who, if they wanted to float, had to clear their pond of debris, which amounted to a good deed.

When I was an adolescent behaving in irresponsible ways, I had two friends I adored: they were twins, a boy and a girl, their names began with the same letter and almost rhymed. He was feminine and she was masculine, he was lithe and delicate with a high voice while she was muscular with a low, gravelly voice. I was closer to her than to him, but as they were as close as close and always together it hardly made a difference. They were in a band; he played guitar and she played drums. I was not in the band but on Friday nights there was always a party in the basement of the twins' house and the band played, or practiced, which was basically the same thing. When they weren't playing we did things that we thought were outrageously funny, such as throwing breakfast cereal into the toilet bowl and pretending it was vomit. We went to my friends' house because their mother was a widow and every Friday night she went on a date, leaving the house to us. We would party, and though I no longer remember what that feels like, I know it involves a desperate need to forget something. At around midnight their mother would come home so drunk she had to be put to bed by her children, and often I would help them get her up on the bed and out of her shoes. We didn't think anything of it, obviously she had partied while we were partying and that's what Friday nights were for. This went on for two years and then my family moved away and I had new friends and went to a new school. But judging from the journals I kept then, my sole purpose in life was to find a way to get back to my old friends. Reading the journals it is quite clear I was in love, though I have no memory of feeling this way. We wrote letters for a few years, but by the time I graduated from high school we had lost touch altogether. Years later—I was in my fifties—I came across a box of their baby pictures and pictures of their early childhood. It seemed to me I had so many pictures of them that they must have none, and I wanted to return the pictures but hadn't a clue as to where the twins lived.

Somewhere in Texas, I thought. I called information in Dallas, I called information in Houston, and then I gave up. The pictures meant nothing to me, they just took up space, so I threw them all out. And then about a year later my phone rang and it was her. She had found me. We talked for about thirty minutes—military, disability, cabin in the woods, dogs, mother had gotten sober and married a great guy but was dead now—and promised to stay in touch. I knew what would happen next: the phone rang and it was her brother, she had called him immediately after talking to me. So I chatted with him—military, commercial pilot, never married—and said goodbye. I didn't mention the pictures. The next day I got another call from his sister, inviting me to their high school reunion; I reminded her that I didn't go to high school with them, it had been junior high, but she said it didn't matter because she and her brother organized the reunion every year and could invite anyone they wanted and I wouldn't regret it because it was a blast, they rented a Ramada Inn in Dallas and partied for two days, a whole weekend, it was *the* event of the year, they lived for it, everyone lived for it, I would love it, it was a *blast*. I told her I didn't go to my own high school reunion, that I was not the "reunion type," that I was very busy anyway and didn't like to travel. She would not take no for an answer and called week after week begging me to come party in Texas. Finally I stopped answering the phone. She kept calling, I didn't pick up, and finally she stopped. I think she understood I was somehow not the same, I was not the same as I was at thirteen and I was not the same as they were now. I felt bad about the pictures, though; I don't really know how I came to have them, it must have been we were partying and the family album came out and either I stole them (because I was in love) or they were wantonly given away.

But in the photographs my friends were so innocent, little children on tricycles or holding Easter baskets, and it saddened me to think of them as adults, having a blast in the Ramada Inn once a year; it fairly broke my heart, but then again I was just as sad over myself—look who I had become, having destroyed without thinking the childhood memories of another, just sitting there at my desk ripping the photos up, tossing them into the basket beneath me.

I have a friend whom I have never met; I am pretty sure we will meet next year because two of the friends I've written about here have died since writing this.

I have a friend I met once and only briefly and we have corresponded ever since. In the beginning, we wrote long letters using words, but for some years now we have not; now we exchange, by mail, flowering branches, birds' nests, tiny gloves, feather hats, and once she sent me the entire sweepings from her porch—shards of blue clapboard paint mixed with dirt, leaves, and debris: beauty by accident, as so many friendships are.

I have a friend who wishes she were not a human animal but an animal with fur. A fox, a dog, or a rabbit. This disturbs me so much I love her even more.

I have a friend I have known for fifty years. She is the purest poet I know, but she has not written a poem since she was twenty; instead she has chosen, day after day, to wear only blue or gray, and I consider this an ingenious, even perfect, solution to the problem of poetry and time.

I had a friend I loved for twenty-five years, and then the earth opened between us, and now we have not spoken in twenty-five years. But nearly every week I dream of her, so there is this sense, for me at least, that we still know and love each other, but only late in the night, behind closed eyes.

I have a friend who did "exactly the opposite of what one would have expected from the first" (as Proust says in a letter) and when this was done, my last beliefs in the architecture of reason and coherence were completely demolished, and as for the inevitable debris found among the ruins, I blew that away myself, though not as easily as one dispels a bit of dust. Thus I have a friend I love but do not trust and never will.

I had a friend who was only briefly my friend, he was the friend of a friend and I knew him for only two months while I was working on the West Coast, but one afternoon he performed an act of kindness that has flowered in me for half a century. When picking me up from work, merely giving me a ride home, he stood across the street with a brown paper bag in his hand, and in the bag was a muffin he had bought for me, no more than that, and yet at nineteen it was the greatest act anyone had ever performed in front of me—a muffin in a bag for a girl too sad and too young to say she was sad, to tell anyone, yet here he was, my friend, lifting and waving the bag from across the street. How do you thank someone for something like that? You don't, half a century passes, and even if you did they would think you were a lunatic, but you are not a lunatic because someone once gave you a muffin in a brown bag, assuring you that you were sane, and would be, forever.

I had a friend who, at a very sad time in my life, was more or less my only friend, and she was sad, too, and she was a dog. She was not my dog, I had never had a dog, I knew nothing about dogs, I had heard they were "man's best friend" but thought that was sentimental and without weight. My friend belonged to a very young couple—too young to be a couple, in my opinion—who lived in the apartment below mine. They fought all the time, especially at night. They screamed and hollered at each other and sounded a lot like an old married couple who fought, which is why I thought they were way too young to live like that. My friend, the dog, used to visit me when her parents (masters, owners?) fought; I would hear her scratching at my door, she couldn't bark because her vocal cords had been removed by her original owner (parent, master?). Her hips had been damaged in an accident and she wore a brace around her hind. I could hear her scratching at my door with her front paw and I would let her in, together we would sit and listen to the fighting coming up through the floor, she would be trembling and I would put my arms around her and we would stay like that for the longest time. I always had food and water for her, she knew right where they were on the floor, and since at that time I myself was eating very little on account of my sadness, I would eat a little something from my cupboard when she ate. So we would eat together and hold each other, and then her master (parent, owner?) would holler for her to come down and she would go, I would hold the door open for her and she would turn one last time to look at me before she limped down the stairs. She could not bark or whimper or make the least sound. I loved her. One day I put a silly cardboard frame over her head so that it sat on her neck and framed her face and I took her picture. The whole thing lasted no more than a minute, and today, thirty years later, her portrait still sits by my desk. I know she is dead but I don't know how the last years of her life turned out—one night the couple had an explosive fight, my friend came upstairs to sit with me, and in the morning her mother (owner, master?) packed the car and left, taking my friend with her. As I stood in the parking lot I could not bring myself to say goodbye, I didn't hug her or pet her, I just looked at her and walked inside. If she had anything to say she couldn't say it, nor could I. But I could cry and that was a blessing. Now when I think of dogs I understand that the relationship *is* very sentimental, and carries great and lasting weight, like any friendship.

I have a friend, and for several years we were both lost at the same time, at loose ends, adrift. He lived on the West Coast and I lived on the East Coast, and many nights we talked for hours on the phone, keeping each other company. Even the long silences were comfortable between us, but some of the things we said to each other were so strange I began writing them down, writing things down was everything to me and it was everything to him, someone who knew us well said we could complete each other's sentences, and that was true too. He would say "I can't talk to people who don't know what they are doing" when it was clear neither of us knew what we were doing. Once he said "I'm so slow," and I said "I know, you have a head of butter and a body of water," which he pretty much does, and another time he said "L. is so much smarter than I am . . . no, not smarter but . . . he has a wife." Then we would crack up and the minutes flew. Suddenly he would exclaim "Look at this, a helicopter! What would Kafka say?" He was always reporting on things happening outside his window—once he saw a mountain lion—while out my window I saw only squirrels. A dear friend of his died, and his wistful comment was "I am completely unable to make myself stutter." He was that smooth, butter and water. Then he lost another friend, suddenly and unexpectedly, and he said "No one knows what to say. That's why poetry exists." I was contemplating getting an aquarium, a large one, and his reaction was "You have to have a sense of irony to buy a gigantic aquarium in the first place, but once you start sitting in front of it and staring you've lost your sense of irony." We would always talk about what we were having, or just had, for dinner. I'd say "I just ate a plump little hand-fed hand-raised chicken, isn't that sad?" and he'd respond "I don't want to upset you because you've already upset yourself, but all I ate today was cardboard." Another conversation went like this: "Sorry, I'm just me these days"; "That's your problem, you're just you so snap out of it!" I would hear his doorbell ring in the background and he would say "That's my dry cleaning being delivered." To me that was insanely indulgent, but he would remind me that his family were immigrants and say "We didn't come to this country to change lightbulbs," then I'd remind him that they came to this country because we *have* lightbulbs. It was just banter, completely idle, and we loved it. We could say anything to each other, and that is one of the great gifts of friendship. We shared a wavelength, and we still do, though our lives are no longer adrift and we don't talk nearly so often, but the sound of his voice is as familiar to me as air. We often spoke out of the blue, without any context, and once he said something totally unexpected, he said "Women are incredible. I just wanted to say that, in case any women are listening."

I have a friend who is the best-read human being I have ever known; not only has he read everything you have ever heard of, read, or hoped to read, he has read novels like *The Mysteries of Udolpho* and *Penguin Island*, he has read *Lorna Doone*, he has read *The Exegesis of Philip K. Dick*, he has read Duns Scotus, his idol is David Hume, and although he is completely indifferent towards Shakespeare, my friend is also the sanest person I know. Eccentric and sane, a dynamo combination. He has a beautiful, compassionate wife whom he adores, two beautiful grown children whom he adores, and he lives in a modest home that is one of the warmest and most welcoming I have ever been in. Yet his special place is in its basement, where he has a grotto, his refuge, his private sanctuary. This room is cold and damp and covered floor to ceiling with shelves holding his collections, which include a hundred porcelain figurines on whose faces unusual expressions have been caught, framed photographs of forgotten movie stars, a hundred peculiar ashtrays, a thousand tiny matchbooks, and everything in between. It resembles an antique store of the particular kind that a fetish-minded customer would buy out on the spot. A foreign director once wanted to film it, but my friend declined. This is where he keeps his books, and his postcards—of which he has over twenty thousand—arranged in metal filing cabinets. In middle age he suffered the proverbial collapse, after which he became a serious student of Buddhism, meditating daily in his grotto. He was born a Jew, the son of Holocaust survivors who so traumatized his development that their level of control and his level of guilt constantly collided—his mother would not allow him to wear worn, frayed jeans in high school because she didn't survive for her son to wear rags—and eventually he became not a misanthrope but a slightly misanthropic man, having learned early on through books and life that inhumanity is an ongoing reality.

If "history teaches, but it has no pupils" (Gramsci), my friend is sitting in that otherwise empty classroom. Yet over the years his wife and family, his music, his dog, have brought him such genuine solace and love that he considers himself a fortunate man. One day I said to him his whole philosophy could be summed up in a sentence, *Life is terrible, terrible, and I am a fortunate man*. He laughed with acknowledgment. But sometime later it dawned on me that my friend, who had spent his whole life escaping the clutch of his parents, had finally come to a summation that was in effect theirs, for they had drummed into him since he first gasped for air that life was terrible and he was fortunate. Which is my philosophy entirely, for life *is* terrible, and I *am* fortunate, fortunate to have such a friend, who keeps me ever aware and in check, as on the day he said to me from out of the blue *oh, are you so cozy in your life you can turn down a red-flocked bear ashtray?*

I have a friend who died, yet every time I think of him I smile, and am never sad. How can you not smile when you recall a man who, given the choice, would only eat white food? His favorite meal, which he often served to guests, was boiled spaghetti with cheese sprinkled on top, cheese you shook from a can, and for dessert a boxed Boston cream pie with the chocolate glaze diligently scraped off. A man who was such a romantic his idea of a pickup line was "You have all the colors of October in your hair, come and have a doughnut in my car." He also dumped a bucket of sand on the floor of his car so he could "take the beach with him" wherever he went. A masterful writer who had published to acclaim but fell out with the times and in his dotage announced with glee that a few paragraphs were appearing in *Yankee* magazine.

Someone who recited Shelley and Keats in the middle of a conversation about pudding. A man who was determined to tap a maple tree for syrup, and upon tapping the lone spindly tree in his front yard announced with pride that a cup of sap had produced a teaspoon of syrup that he gave as a gift to his neighbor's dog. The last time I saw my friend was the night of a full moon when he desired us to view it from the end of a pier so dangerously dilapidated it had been cordoned off by a chain and an ordinance. He drove to the chain, got out of his car, unhitched the chain, and drove us to the end of the pier where we sat in silence as the moon rose over the ocean. Finally he turned to me and said *they can't keep the moon out*.

I have a friend I have known since the day she was born. She is not my daughter, or my sister, but the daughter of a friend, at least she was the daughter of my friend for the first twenty years of her life before she became a *friend*, my friend. This came as a surprise to me, I had never considered that someone you knew before she could feed herself would one day be having dinner with you, holding a fork. If we are at the movies and go to the ladies' room together I don't think of her as being in diapers, though she once was and I knew her then. It is a mysterious thing how one person becomes another, and I cherish her friendship as utterly distinct from any others I have. But because she is thirty-five years younger than I am, and in all probability I will die before she reaches her full adulthood—before she is my age—I sometimes feel like a wild duck flying over her head, knowing all the time we have spent together will one day be no more than an occasional vivid memory for her (unlike a parent, whom one thinks of constantly). And then I realize that this is true of all friendships—they are wild ducks flying overhead—and that my friendship with her is no different than any other, and therefore perfect.

I had a friend I had known for years but we never lived in the same place at the same time, and then we did. For six months we lived in the same city and had dinner every week on the same night in the same restaurant at the same time at the same table and ordered the same thing (wild mushrooms in cream sauce) and drank the same wine (Sancerre). During dinner he told me the story of his life in increments, dinner by dinner, like a serialized novel. They were wonderful dinners and because we were moving from his birth to the present, and because the story of a heterosexual stockbroker who becomes a bisexual surrealist poet is a long one, we were always the last to leave the restaurant, the staff came to know us and let us linger at our table while they prepared to close for the night. My friend and I were doing the same work but because he was paid twice what I was he insisted on paying and would never let me pick up the bill. He did agree that I could pay for our last dinner and that on that occasion we would go somewhere new. Because I wanted to repay him in any way I could I chose an even more expensive restaurant, a Japanese one that was written up in all the papers. It was terrible. The food was so minimal we would look at our plates and make up ridiculous haiku on the spot, staring at a shred of vegetable floating in water. There were a hundred kinds of sake and we tried a great many of them, giving them titles. Haunted Bell. Chrysanthemum Tragedy. Nightingale Hit by a Fan. As the night wore on the names grew increasingly Western and literary until we were drinking Forlorn Incubus, and Apropos of Wet Snow. Shared misery can be a joy. I saw my friend once more before he died—we had dinner in a foreign country—and we spent that dinner talking about all our other dinners. Dinner with friends, it doesn't get any better than that. When you eat dinner with friends, the ones you really love and no other, you have reached a pinnacle you don't see, but it is there. Look around the table—"*in the still garden the meal shines for a gathering of friends*"—and if someone starts clearing it, put your hand on their arm ever so lightly, ever so briefly, pause that plate in midair.

I had a friend when I was ten, and she was a Mormon. We played together after school and on the weekends, and one night her mother invited me to stay for dinner. It was a large family, and they sat at a round table, and when it was time to say grace each one of them folded their arms in front of their chest, which startled me, as that was something my mother did when she was angry, when she stood in the kitchen and let you know. We said grace in my family, but we folded our hands together and bowed our heads, and no one could ever tell who was angry and who was not. When I ate with my friend's family, I thought they were all angry with God, and it confused me. Why would you pray when you were angry with God? I was too polite to ask my friend why Mormons did this, so for a long time it stewed in me. I had another friend at that time who was also Mormon, and one day she took me to her basement and showed me what her family kept down there—huge burlap sacks of lentils and beans and rice. She said this was the food her family would live on when there was an apocalypse. I asked her what an apocalypse was and she said it was an event that would cause the whole planet to explode and burn. I did not understand why anyone would want to survive such a thing but was too polite to say so. Then I remembered the

Mormons were angry when they prayed, and why not, they had to survive in ashes and live on beans. Suddenly I understood and things began to make sense to me, at the age of ten, thanks to my friends.

I had a friend in high school who was not my best friend but she lived closest to me in the city and it was easy to walk to her house on the weekends. She lived in a house and I lived in an apartment. Her family was sophisticated in ways that were new and mysterious to me. Her father, I found out years later, was a CIA agent whose cover was working as a cultural attaché with an emphasis in Asian art. These were the "days of Vietnam," as we refer to them now, which sounds so peculiar in retrospect, as if a fad for straw or silk had swept through the country. My friend's mother came from a wealthy Southern family and had once been a professional ballerina, a fact that deeply impressed me, as even my English teacher (and I excelled in English) told me I was a *klutz* without a single bodily grace belonging to any of the nine muses. He had been watching me through a classroom window as I tried, on the court below, to hit a tennis ball. Later he went so far as to insult my clothing, telling me to my face my dress was ridiculous, and so it was, a brown shift with huge turquoise polka dots, a Peter Pan collar and a big floppy bow. My sister had made it, she made all my clothes. We weren't allowed to wear pants to school. My friend's sister took fencing lessons in a white bodysuit; she had a *saber* and a *grilled mask*. It was all too much. My friend had several fur coats that were so odd and interesting you couldn't guess what animal they were made from. I joked once that she was wearing her monkey coat. It occurs to me now that it probably *was* a monkey coat, as monkeys can be found in all the Asian countries her father, supposedly collecting the antique heads of Buddha, traveled to. So that was the situation. My mother adored my friend, she liked my friend better than any of my other friends because when meeting my mother for the first time my friend had *curtsied.* I think my mother had waited her whole life for that moment. My mother loved fruit. I think she would as soon have married a pear as my father. There was always a big bowl of fruit in the kitchen. Liver-spotted bananas, and green grapes as translucent as jade, though if I ate the grapes, the arthritic stems that remained terrified me, I imagined them as crippled hands coming to get me. And there were always apples, her favorite. In those days there weren't *kinds* of apples, you couldn't say "I feel like a Gala," or "Pick up some Granny Smiths," there were only, well, apples. They were red, all shaped the same, and perfectly tasteless. My mother kept another bowl of fruit in the dining room, and all of that fruit was artificial. When I was younger it was plastic but by the time I was in high school it had all turned to bone china. In my mother's mind, there was a very big difference between a plastic orange and an orange made from china, and if you couldn't tell the difference you had no taste, none at all. It was the difference between a handshake and a curtsy. Years and years later, I wrote a poem and in the poem are the passing words *a world where no one ever even curtsies anymore.* And I have noticed through the years that many readers want, even demand, a backstory to anything that is ever written, and now I have given them *the entire backstory* of these fleeting words, and I feel for a moment like my friend, who curtsied in front of my mother, something my mother had always wanted, and got once.

When I walk through a city I see many strange faces, and though none leave a trace I know they have friends. Who are their friends, whose friends are they? For wherever I walk, images of my friends go with me.

I have a friend who used to be a dancer. She once choreographed and performed a dance I have never forgotten. She danced to Al Green singing "How Can You Mend a Broken Heart." She was solo on the stage, and a spotlight followed her as she moved. She was wearing a paper bodysuit, and as she moved the paper tore, at first in tiny slits at the seams, and then in big gashes, rip after rip until she was dancing in shreds, practically naked. It was so bold and beautiful and sad, and happened once and once only; it was something to behold, and then it vanished from the earth.

LETTER TO ELIZABETH BISHOP

Dear Elizabeth,

Margot, whom you have never met, says that my outfit is one you would not be caught dead in, but as you *are* dead, I am of the surest that you would be happy to be seen alive in it, if you could. I am writing you from Saratoga Springs, New York and it is not even the coldest spring but the worst February, the light is not strong enough to walk across the room. We are here celebrating your life and letters and I suppose the poems are the most of it but they celebrate themselves and I am not here to say anything about that, however I know you will be interested in the things that have changed, poetry not being among them, but when one is of a certain age and has thought all night about death, one eventually realizes that one wants not to die not because of never seeing one's beloveds again—shameful as that is—but because one wonders what the cars will look like, what assassinations will happen and where and when, how all manner of things in and of themselves will change, the shape of objects, newer and newer food, and shoes and hats and such, all the stuff of the world, the thingness. For instance there is a substance called velcro, a kind of cloth with the raised texture of a baby porcupine, one whose quills have not quite hardened, and two pieces of this cloth, when held together, create a bond, eliminating the need for zippers, buttons, laces, and ties. One would think we had an abiding human need for and interest in buttons and laces but apparently not, things go the way of things the way the flesh goes the way of flesh. Oh Elizabeth I am sorry to say we are also now living in the End of the Age of Paper, another substance that is fast afloat downstream in the direction of some final extinction. This will be hard for you to believe, yet remember the letter you once wrote (not to me; your letters, you will be aghast to hear, have gone and gotten themselves published, I don't know whom to blame)—well, in one letter you said, writing from Brazil to Boston, that if you did not own a Black Watch plaid wool blazer you would positively *die*, and you sent a little picture of one in the letter and asked them to send you one right away, enclosing, presumably, enough money to cover the cost of the blazer and its postage to the southern hemisphere: well, I saw two days ago, in a jumble heap of woolens at the thrift store, Charity Shop to you, a very long woolen scarf—at least three feet long—of Black Watch plaid, made in Scotland, the match to your jacket. And I did not buy it, though I toyed with the idea in your honor, no, Elizabeth, I left it there in the dirty heap. Why? Because the Age of the Black Watch Plaid has passed, no one wears it anymore, you would not be caught dead in it, even if you were alive. It is as charming as ever, that plaid, but its existence harks back to the time before women alive today existed. Why does it still exist, you may ask, and it exists precisely because it is useless, like all beautiful things Elizabeth, your poems and jacket among them, they persist in their secret obscurity, they go on and on wearing the shoes of a ghost who

THE GABLES

We came to The Gables for the first night of our engagement. I told my fiancé this is *exactly* what I want our bedroom to look like! I have never seen a headboard that thrilled me so. Pillows with chocolate on them, flowers in the fireplace, towels folded in the shape of swans—and a journal next to the bed, so I can tell him how I feel! As I lie here on this magnificent bed I surely know this is how Empress Alexandra felt in her mauve boudoir—of course she was married to the Czar of Russia but I know this is the relaxing luxury she received—plus I was in Vermont! "We shall return," as the General said, how could we not?

I think it was all part of God's plan—to give us a warm bath with many bubbles. To make us a King & Queen. So while the usual haste of romantic passion was spent slumbering, our stay could not have been more peaceful. We were King & Queen filled with attention to detail. Thank you.

(The Gables was the first place my Lady stayed in the United States and I know she will always remember it. The adjectives could fill a book. I'm sure no one ever came close to our first experience. It was one of the most beautiful October nights I have ever seen, here in our beautiful room. Merci!)

This is the first time my husband and I have spent the night away from our infant son. It was wonderful! It was so quiet here, at one point we went outside just to hear some background noise.

It is my job to be professionally spoiled. We are back for the third time.

Heaven in an ice bucket!

The Lord told us to come here and gave my husband many dreams and confirmations about The Gables. What place other than a castle would the King have his children stay? This weekend is simply a celebration of the ménage à trois of us three: the Lord, my husband, and me.

Forever will I remember this night into the days of longevity.

11:45, only 15 minutes left in the greatest day of my life.

The Gables is an inspiration that creates a new illusion of life! Thank you for that.

The atmosphere here demands relaxation.

It was so nice not having to worry about anything except what we were going to do next!

The Gables is so beautiful that I have always had a great appreciation for architecture. I would love to stay here again, but our next special occasion will most likely be in Belgium, Japan, or even England.

AFFORDABLE VACATION

Pretend you are a penny, travel as one for two weeks, come home and tell your friends where you have been, where you stayed, what you saw, the people you met and all your adventures. You might not have any pictures, but you came home spent and anyone will be able to see it was a wild vacation, one that makes two weeks in an Italian villa seem boring, yep, everyone agrees you are lucky, your face is shining and you're ready to leave again at a moment's notice.

AN AMERICAN HAIKU

The days were long and the nights even longer. It had been a long time since the last haiku and the haikuist did not know where the next seventeen syllables would come from. When they came they would come unexpectedly, arrive unannounced, he knew that much from his years of experience, yet years of experience counted for very little when it came to haiku. Returning from a recent trip, the smell of Cinnabons in an airport held out the promise of a haiku, but it didn't seem very haikuish in the end. After he boarded his connecting flight he wondered if the suddenly vanishing smell wasn't perhaps more haikuish than the first whiff, but a haiku should not be a memory, it should be endlessly occurring, and so he further nixed the sound of the car wheels rumbling over the highway when, as a child, he had slept on the floor in the back of his family's car, his face so close to the road—separated, really, by only an inch or two of metal—that the sound of the powerful motion beneath him seemed to him, a mere five-year-old, to be the heartbeat of another world, a world he could not quite enter, though he be inches from it. After the haikuist returned from his journey, the only memorable part being the smell of Cinnabons baking in the airport, he resumed his daily life, shopping for food at the supermarket where, on a flagpole, a gigantic American flag was rippling in slow motion over the parking lot, moved by the March wind, backlit almost to transparency by the March light, and this sight struck him as suitable for a haiku, but no sooner had he parked than the idea vanished. Coming home he drove past the local thrift store, where in the window hung a very old wedding dress next to an old blue suitcase, and he almost stopped, thinking he had found his haiku, or it had found him, but he drove on home. At home he made an important phone call to a government agency and was put on hold for forty-two minutes while the agency played Muzak full of static. He sat mindlessly eating chips from a bag which crumbled and crunched as he emptied it, as if the bag itself were one big chip, and these forty-two minutes on hold he mentally tried to reduce to seventeen syllables (including the chips) but when his patience paid off and an actual government agent addressed him, he forgot all about his haiku. His conversation with the agent was frustrating, and afterwards, to relieve his stress, he drove to the local swimming pool. Submerged in the lap lane, every time he turned his head underwater he had a view of the legs of the weak and elderly in the therapy lane, all sizes and shapes of legs were slowly pumping underwater, and the haikuist was so moved by the sight he was determined to write a haiku capturing the moment, but then he felt guilty, using the weak and elderly as inspiration. He argued with himself for a while, got out of the pool, showered, dressed, and drove home. On the way there he saw a man sitting on the curb at a neighborhood grocery store, the man's head was bent over a lotto card and he was scratching at it with a coin. It almost looked like he was writing, and the haikuist was reminded of himself—when would *he* get lucky and write his next haiku? It had been more than a month. A month filled with many haikuish moments, to the extent he was beginning to think of one long haiku, rising and subsiding like waves in the ocean, coming forward and dropping a seashell, which, whenever the haikuist picked it up, he put to his ear and heard again the long road rolling away beneath him when as a child he slept on the floor of his parent's car. Then the sea took the shell back.

TEETH OF NOON

When I was nineteen I enrolled in a college in the Swiss Alps. It had once been a sanatorium such as Thomas Mann describes in *The Magic Mountain*. Every dorm room had a balcony overlooking the Dents du Midi, the Teeth of Noon, seven jagged snow-covered peaks. Nabokov lived down the mountain in a hotel on a lake with swans. Nearer than that was the Château de Chillon, where Byron and Shelley stopped one summer afternoon while sailing together. In the afternoon I'd sit on my balcony wrapped in a blanket, reading. Whenever I looked up, there were the Teeth of Noon sparkling at me. Down the hall was the old operating theater, larger than the average dorm room, so that six girls roomed there together. They were my friends and I spent a lot of time in the operating theater, just hanging out, lying on the bunks. One day a rumor flew there was going to be a drug raid that evening, I had half a pound of hashish hidden under my bed so I had no choice but to eat it all before the raid, which never happened. That same evening I was playing a hooker in a Sartre play and forgot all my lines. I just made stuff up, and thus ended that career. Down the road was an extraordinary pastry shop and an English bookstore, for the English had been coming to the village for a long time and enjoyed sweets and reading. And the local fire brigade needed to practice their drill on the sanatorium, which was ten stories high, so they asked for volunteers to go up on the roof and slide down a canvas shoot into the arms of a fireman. I was the first to volunteer and slid down the canvas shoot into the arms of a Swiss firefighter. Oh my life was dreary, my whole existence bored me, so I suddenly decided to drop out and left school without telling my parents or anyone else, except my psychology teacher, who came to my room and asked me did I want to talk to someone before I made such a rash decision. I said no, my mind was made up, it was strong and clear. I was young, I wanted so much more. Like Youth Itself I did not grasp I was living a dream of exhilarating newness. I walked away, I said goodbye to the Teeth of Noon and began my bewildered life.

THE EFFUSIVE

It's been a great year. I turned seventy and my brother shot himself. I am a tall person who is small and mean inside. For instance, on Christmas morning I wake and begin to pack away all my Christmas decorations. I love Christmastime (December 1–24) but I hate the glare of Christmas morning, the sound of crumpling wrapping paper, and the belief that it is still actually Christmas. I like to get a head start on things, which is why I am constantly planning for death. I throw away birthday cards on the morning of my birthday. In seventy years I have read a great many books but I do not remember—cannot tell you—a single sentence or line from any of them. It seems to me I am merely a walking trunk of titles. I would rather read a children's book than cook. Yet I believe I am a genuine person, an ordinary, normal creature who loves flowers unless they are yellow, though wild yellow tulips grow rampant in the woods next to my house and I like them so much one year I picked a bunch only to discover they wither instantly when picked. *Never hit a child or pick a wildflower* is ancient wisdom, passed on for so long it has finally disappeared. I find this sad, now that I have learned my lesson. I was beaten when I was a child, but like Christmas morning so what to all that. Nothing stops my life from moving forward towards my death. I hate chocolate (the people who love me keep giving it to me, even if I put it in writing they will not stop). I hate parties of all kinds, and give two magnificent ones every year. One is at Christmas, and one is in the spring when the wild yellow tulips are in bloom. My guests and I, we sit in silence and stare at the tulips through the trees, it is a genuine moment of feeling sad that we can't pick them, knowing we should not, and understanding they will wither whether or not they are picked.

THE NOVEL

I was reading in front of the fire, it was a luxury, it was snowing outside, bitterly cold, but there in my snuggling I was on fire with my book, a recently published novel that had been translated into over twenty languages, I was in the middle of a sentence when a thought of my own intruded—somewhere in the world someone else was reading the same novel and was in sync with my own reading, reading the same sentence I was, and I was gripped with this knowledge and with fear and terror—I had thought I was alone but someone else was reading with me, the same sentence, apace with me, word by word my terror spread, I wanted to be the only one reading, to be in the middle of *a solitary act*, that is why I had built the fire in the first place, why I had lain down on the couch in front of the fire, but I was not, unquestionably I was not the only one reading this book at this moment, and I was so utterly de-selved, so turned around and so tortured I stopped reading, I stood up and commanded myself to walk, I told myself that the other reader would be going on ahead, ahead and alone, we would no longer be synchronized and I could again be an individual with individual pursuits, I walked around the room with my pulse beating, my heart racing, I tried to calm myself, I said to myself *this is ridiculous*, and then I lay down again and began to read, safe in the knowledge that the other reader was at least a page ahead of me, what a relief, I did not have to share my moment-to-moment experience with him—or her—or they—in Tashkent or Paris, Granada or Stuttgart—and I kept reading, I was calm, I forgot about my irrational fears of a moment ago, and some hundred pages on, when they were entirely forgotten, the author began writing about the fear of the doppelgänger, the twin, the mirror, the echo, the identical other, and I was paralyzed again, not with fear of the other reader, who was by now pages and pages ahead of me, but with the new fear that the author inhabited me, and had my thoughts, and that my experience was no longer my own, and never had been.

THE BOOK

That book sat on my various shelves for decades until I got around to it, and then it seemed to be written especially for me. I hope this provides some hope to the other unread books surrounding me who are wondering what will happen to them when I die. I don't have the heart to tell them they will all be sold or recycled and will never see one another again. I think we do books an injustice by cramming them so closely together on shelves. A certain intimacy inevitably occurs and when they find themselves separated and stickered with a new price that underscores their loneliness, there is little that a new reader can do to ameliorate their sorrow but to read them and say *Old Friend, you were written especially for me.*

CHILLY OBSERVATION

Do you know the story of the woman who went to a taverna in Greece, her table was set on the beach, after a while the tide came in, the water covered her legs and the legs of the table and the waiter continued to serve her, going back and forth from the kitchen as if nothing were happening? People often wonder what it is like to be old, and a few actually ask.

THE PLUM AND THE DEVIL

This plum sat in the sun for three hours, its skin split apart and its syrup began to ooze out. When I bit into it I thought of William Carlos Williams, and I thought of Anne Frank, who had a can of sardines thrown to her over a barbed-wire fence but another prisoner caught it and ran away. And I thought of the three or four blank pages between her last diary writing and her unfinished novel, which she had begun by turning the account-book, the one she was currently using, upside down and writing forward from the back. I thought of things upside down, I thought of how Williams's plum was cold and mine was warm, the sun and the icebox. I thought of the blank pages separating the child from the writer. As if in a few years they would meet. I bit into the plum, it was the most delicious plum I had ever eaten, it was July ninth, 2022, and I thought of the line *How paltry is the Devil's power to destroy compared to what can momentarily be*. The plum, the plum! But what about the novel?

What is it, the heart,
is it the sound of the pine trees
blowing in the painting?

Notes

"My Memory of a Story by Lydia Davis I Read Years Ago and *Never Forgot*": This was simply a personal exercise in literary memory, one I failed in every way. But it proved what I have always suspected—we remember nothing of what we have read and loved, only that we loved it. Love is what remains of our reading life. Try it yourself, and good luck!

"Letter to Elizabeth Bishop": Some years ago I was asked to take part in an art show centered on Elizabeth Bishop; all I had to do was sit at a table and type, using an old black heavy typewriter. As she must have. It was a one-day event and I think the gallery was open about four hours. I remember I wore close-fitting slacks, a turtleneck sweater, and ballet flats, thinking I looked circa 1959. I typed several letters to friends to whom I owed a letter and then I was at a loss and decided to write Elizabeth. This piece, unabridged, ends in the middle of a sentence because the gallery was closing and I was eager to stop, stand up, and go home.

"The Gables": Often when I travel I am lodged in a B and B, and often by the side of the bed there are blank journals where guests are welcome to write their impressions of the place; this piece is a compilation of some of those entries. I have made a few changes.

Acknowledgments

THE MOST OF IT

Thanks to the editors of the following journals, in which many of these pieces first appeared: *The Alaska Quarterly Review*, *Blue Mesa Review*, *Conjunctions*, *Cue*, *Harper's*, *The Iowa Review*, *jubilat*, *Mississippi Review*, *The Seneca Review*, *Sentence*, *The Southern Review*, *Spoon River Poetry Review*, *Third Coast*, and *TriQuarterly*.

"The Bench" appears courtesy of Carnegie Mellon University Press.

"A Romantic Poet and His Destiny" is slightly altered from a text I found on a paper placemat in a diner off Interstate 91. The poet described is Heinrich Heine (1797–1856). I was served a hamburger on top of this, and had to ask the waitress for a clean "copy" of the mat. I have no idea who wrote it, but I admired its succinctness, for I happened to be reading a five-hundred-page biography of Heine.

MY PRIVATE PROPERTY

I am grateful to the editors of the following magazines and journals, where many of these pieces first appeared or were reprinted: *The Best American Poetry*, *Diagram*, *Ecotone*, *The Fabulist*, *Granta*, *Harper's*, *The Hoot & Hare Review*, *The Kenyon Review*, *The Lumberyard*, *MAKE: A Literary Magazine*, *Matrix*, *Music & Literature*, *The Paris Review*, *Storyscape*, *Tin House*, and *Unstuck*.

* Author's note: In each of the color pieces, if you substitute the word *happiness* for the word *sadness*, nothing changes.

THE BOOK

Some of these pieces have appeared in *The Arkansas International*, *FIELDNOTES*, *The Glacier*, *Granta*, *Jung Journal*, *Mississippi Review*, *Passages North*, *The Poetry Review* (London), *The Sewanee Review*, and *Then Again: Vintage Photography Reimagined by One Artist and Thirty-One Writers*.

The epigraph by Francis Jammes is translated by Bruce Whiteman.

The opening of "Golden Crumbs" comes from English novelist Florence Warden (1857–1929).

The opening of "The Book" is taken verbatim from a letter my friend Lawrence Sutin wrote me.

The line in italics at the end of "The Plum and the Devil" is by Jack Gilbert.

This book is printed with plant-based inks on materials
certified by the Forest Stewardship Council®. The FSC®
promotes an ecologically, socially and economically
responsible management of the world's forests.
This book has been printed without
the use of plastic-based coatings.

The authorized representative in the EEA
is eucomply OÜ, Pärnu mnt 139b-14,
11317 Tallinn, Estonia.
hello@eucompliancepartner.com
+337 576 90241

Fitzcarraldo Editions
133 Rye Lane,
London, SE15 4ST
United Kingdom

Originally published in the United States by Wave Books
First published in the United Kingdom
by Fitzcarraldo Editions in 2026

ISBN 978-1-80427-282-4

Design by Ray O'Meara
Typeset in Fitzcarraldo
Printed and bound by Pureprint

fitzcarraldoeditions.com

Fitzcarraldo Editions